MW01005045

The Inheritance

The Haunting Of Lakeside

James M. Matheson

Aberdeenshire Publishing

Phoenix, Arizona

Copyright © 2017 by **James M. Matheson**

Aberdeenshire Publishing
Box 1306
Litchfield Park, Arizona 85340
www.jamesmmatheson.com

Publisher's Note: This is a work of fiction. Names, characters, places, and incidents are a product of the author's imagination. Locales and public names are sometimes used for atmospheric purposes. Any resemblance to actual people, living or dead, or to businesses, companies, events, institutions, or locales is completely coincidental.

The Inheritance. James M. Matheson. -- 1st ed.

Dedicated to Walter B. Gibson

CONTENTS

Joni had the knife poised over the turkey sandwich as the phone rang. The noise emanated into the kitchen where she stood, wondering if it was even worth answering. Nobody called the landline phone save for telemarketers. With a small sigh, she placed the knife on the white counter and walked to the doorway where the phone perched on the wall. She grabbed it off its hook and said 'hello?' hoping she didn't sound as annoyed as she really was.

"Hello, I was hoping to speak with Joni Harrison?" a man said on the other end. His voice was low and gruff. Joni imagined him speaking from a brown leather chair and wearing a thick, graying mustache.

"This is she."

"Hello, Mrs. Harrison, my name is Mr. LeFoy. I am Marie Grezembski's attorney," the man said.

Joni stared into the entrance of the family room. Her eyes wandered from one of her daughter's small pink tennis shoes to the large squares of sunlight that shown onto the light green carpet. She felt dread and uncertainty flow into the pit of her stomach.

"My Aunt Marie? Is everything alright?" Joni asked, knowing full well it wasn't.

"I'm afraid that Mrs. Grezembski passed away on Thursday, Mrs. Harrison. The gardener had come to trim the bushes when he saw your aunt on the floor through the window. He called 911, but unfortunately it was too late. I'm so sorry to be the one to deliver the news to you," the man murmured quietly.

Joni clutched at the white plastic phone, at a loss for words. She pictured her aunt lying against a cold wood floor, the fringes of the terrycloth bathrobe she always wore sticking out at odd angles around her body. She had died alone. Joni ran a hand across her cheeks.

"Thank you for your call and for your condolences, Mr. LeFoy," she spoke into the phone. "I do appreciate it."

The older man cleared his throat. Joni imagined him shifting around uncomfortably in his chair. "I wish that was the only reason why I called, Mrs. Harrison, but unfortunately you are Marie's last living relative. Legally speaking, it is now up to you to handle her affairs and make arrangements."

Joni nodded into the phone, then realized what she had done. "Alright. I will book a flight out for tomorrow morning," she said.

She heard heavy footsteps on the cream tile floor of the kitchen. After a few moments, her husband's face appeared in the doorframe. His straight black eyebrows were crinkled into a frown as he studied his wife's face. Joni's eyes wandered to his now full beard and she absentmindedly told herself that she would need to influence him to trim it soon.

"I greatly appreciate that, Mrs. Harrison," Mr. LeFoy said. His tone was soft and compassionate, making Joni wonder how many similar phone calls he had had to make throughout his career. "Please contact me after you book a flight and we can finalize the details. I have your email address here in front of me, so I will send you my office number, as well as your aunt's address in Ely."

"Okay," Joni replied, fiddling with the white cord of the phone. "Thank you. Goodbye."

She placed the phone back on the hook and turned to face her husband. Tate leaned against the doorway, his arms crossed over his maroon colored plaid shirt. "Is everything alright?" he asked. His lips were spread in an expression of concern.

"No…" she said, tucking a lock of wayward brown hair behind her ear. "My Aunt Marie died. I need to go to Minnesota."

Tate's face melted into a look of sympathy and warmth as he stepped forward and placed his arms around his wife. "Aunt Marie… the romance novelist?" he asked.

Joni nodded into his broad shoulder. "Yes. I need to go pack up her belongings and make arrangements for the funeral. Or cremation? I don't even know," she groaned slightly.

Tate gently lifted her off his shoulder so he could look into her moist hazel eyes. "I can go with you," he said. "I have enough vacation days. You don't have to go alone."

Joni smiled but shook her head. "Adrian is a great brother, but he shouldn't have to take care of his sister for the week or so it will take to get everything finalized. You should stay here with the kids, honey."

Her husband nodded and pulled his wife into his embrace again. "Don't worry about the kids, I'll take care of everything here. Just hurry back home to us as soon as you can."

***

Joni's family dropped her off at the Orlando International Airport the following morning. The Harrisons stood in the large, white lobby as people strode past with luggage of varying sizes. Avery clung to her mother's leg, pleading to go with her as she stared up with wide brown eyes that were uncannily like her father's.

"I'll be back soon," Joni said. "I'll be back within a week or so." She wasn't sure who she was trying to convince more—her daughter or herself.

Fifteen minutes later, Tate was ushering the kids into the backseat of their SUV. Adrian was quiet as he stared at the palm trees that whizzed by. He had already told his mother he would help with Avery, who was ten years his junior. The seven-year-old usually needed help with her homework in the evenings.

Tate did his best to take care of the household while his wife was gone. In the evenings he cooked dinner, spaghetti or chicken or any of the other five meals he knew how to make. Adrian would sit at the kitchen table, hunched over his calculus, as Avery slid around on the tile floor, chatting away about what she and her friends had done at school that day.

It was several days later when Joni called her family, her voice a strange mixture of uncertainty and excitement.

"Has everything been taken care of?" Tate asked, cradling the phone in the crook of his shoulder as he stirred pasta on the stovetop.

"Well, yes, for the most part..." Joni said. "Arrangements for her memorial service and burial are all done. Mr. LeFoy found Aunt Marie's will, and her personal possessions have all been donated to various charities she had written down. There's only one thing I didn't foresee."

Tate let go of the spoon and watched as it continued to twirl with the half-cooked noodles in the pot. His wife had the same tone she adopted when she found a pair of shoes she liked that she knew were too expensive to buy but wanted anyway.

"What's left?" he asked.

"Her house," Joni said. "Lakeside. Her massive, historic house."

"Well, I'm sure your aunt had a substantial mortgage. Her bank can repossess it and put it on the market," Tate reasoned.

"That's the thing," his wife replied. "It's ours now. She left her house to me."

CHAPTER TWO

Two days later Tate sat on their bed with his hands cupped behind his head, watching his wife pace to and fro across their bedroom. The skirt of her blue cotton dress twirled as she pivoted.

"I guess we should have seen this coming," he said, smiling faintly.

Joni threw her hands up. "It never occurred to me!"

"Do you even like your aunt's house?"

Joni stopped mid-stride and plopped down on the edge of the bed. She fingered the cream colored duvet. "Well... there's a lot of woodwork and plum colored wallpaper," she said with a mock grimace.

"It is beautiful, though... and huge," she added.

They were silent for a moment. Through the walls they could hear Avery in her bedroom down the hallway, playing with her dollhouse.

Tate sat up straight and reached for his wife's hand. "Well... the way I see it, we have two options. Either we can put the house on the market and make a decent profit off it, or we can pack our belongings, leave our life in De-land behind and move to Minnesota."

He had said the latter in jest, but as he watched his wife adopt a neutral expression, he realized she considered both options equally possible. "You want to move to Minnesota?" he asked, incredulous.

"No! Yes—I don't know," Joni sighed, nervously playing with his fingers. "I've never considered the idea of leaving Florida before, not once. But this... I don't know. It could be a fresh start for us, for our family."

Tate ran his free hand through his short black hair, making it stand on end. "What would we do there?"

Joni shrugged. "Well... I'm sure you could get another auditing job there. And I was thinking that now that Avery is in school full time, I could finally focus on my career again."

Tate nodded, letting his eyes wander around the room. He looked at the widescreen television they had attached to the wall, and the tall mahogany dresser across from their four poster bed. He tried to imagine these belongings in the confines of a moving truck, in the confines of a new house.

"Interior design, you mean?" he asked, looking back at his wife.

Joni nodded. "It's what I've always wanted to do," she murmured, staring down at the bed again. "I was so excited to start my own design firm, and then we got pregnant with Avery, and everything was put on hold. I don't know why, but this whole house business just makes me realize that it is time for a drastic change. Adrian is going to leave for college soon, and Avery will be a teenager before we know it. It's time for me to focus on what I want to do again, how I can contribute to our family."

Tate swallowed, contemplating her words. He could recall the exact moment they had realized Joni was pregnant. She had emerged from their bathroom with a white plastic stick clutched in her fist. Tate remembered how wide her eyes had been as she stared at him and tossed the pregnancy test to him without a word. He had stared down at that little pink plus sign for ten minutes, uncomprehending.

Tate couldn't imagine not having their vivacious daughter now, but it had certainly thrown a kink into all of their plans. Joni had withdrawn from the design courses she had signed up for and resumed her role as housewife. He looked at his wife seated before him on the bed. Even as she stared down at their blanket, he could see the faintest gleam of excitement in her eyes.

"What is Ely like?" he asked.

Joni's eyes snapped to her husband's, trying to discern what he was thinking. "Well, it's a quiet town," she admitted. "But it was beautiful. The house is right on Shawaga Lake, and the neighbors are all a half mile away or more. The whole place is surrounded by massive, tall trees."

Tate nodded absentmindedly. He began to paint a picture of the place in his mind. He pictured their teenaged son seated by the shore with a Russian novel open in his lap. He imagined Avery running into the lake, squealing in delight as the cold water licked at her legs. And he pictured his wife watching them all from the back deck of Aunt Marie's house, a smile spread across her face.

"Okay," he finally said, and took a deep breath. "Let's move to Minnesota."

Their children, polar opposites in more ways than one, reacted to the news in much the same way as they expected. Joni and Tate had them both sit down at the kitchen table as they discussed their tentative plan. Adrian remained seated, but Avery was instantly on her feet, stomping on the kitchen floor.

"I don't want to move!" she wailed, shaking her head so hard that her purple headband threatened to fall out of her light brown hair. "All of my friends are here in Florida!"

Adrian looked to his little sister with an expression of immense patience. "You'll make new friends, Av," he pointed out, flashing her a quick smile.

Avery squeezed her eyes shut and began to cry, sinking to the floor underneath the table. She pounded her tiny fists against the tiles, blubbering incoherently. Tate eased his body to the floor and stroked her hair as she cried.

Joni and Adrian looked at each other, seated at opposite sides of the white, rectangular table. "How do you feel about the idea? You can be honest," she asked her son.

Adrian flicked his shoulders into a brief shrug. He looked at his mother with hazel eyes, so much like her own. "I'm actually okay with the idea, Mom," he said.

"Ben's father is being relocated, so either way I'm losing my best friend."

"Oh, honey," Joni said, patting his forearm. "I'm so sorry, I didn't know."

Adrian nodded. "It's alright... He found out a couple days ago, so I've gotten used to the idea. I know Minnesota gets cold. Like, ridiculously cold. But the idea of living on a lake sounds pretty enticing."

Joni stared at her seventeen-year-old son, wondering how she had gotten so lucky. Adrian's quiet, serious demeanor had always been a bit of an enigma to her and Tate. They never understood where he had gotten his scholarly attitude, but it was moments like this when she was eternally grateful for it.

She stared down at the table, wincing as Avery continued to wail and writhe on the floor. Adrian smiled at her knowingly. "She'll come around," he whispered. "The moment she makes a friend, she'll come around."

***

The next four weeks flew by in a flurry of activity. Adrian and Avery spent their evenings packing their belongings into boxes. Avery often did so with a scowl on her face, but nevertheless she complied. Tate and Joni took turns flying to Minnesota. Tate handled the paperwork and legalities of selling their Deland house and moving into the new one, while Joni took it upon herself to redecorate their new home.

"I want our house to be a showcase of sorts," she told her husband excitedly. "Nobody is going to hire me as a designer without seeing my skills. I want our new house to be light and fresh… and pretty much nothing like how Aunt Marie had it," she laughed.

Tate had agreed, and had deliberately avoided looking at their joint bank account when he did. His wife had sacrificed so much for their family for so long, and he knew the best thing to do now would be to give her all the support he could—emotionally and financially.

She spent her first day there stripping all of her aunt's gaudy wallpaper off the walls. "Sorry, Marie," she often murmured as she scraped away the varying shades of purple and plum. Her aunt had decorated the house like one of the places you'd find in the pages of the many romance novels she had written. Dark, ornate furnishings, wooden cherubs, and velvet curtains… everything was ostentatious. She wondered how Aunt Marie had lived in the house without feeling compelled to toss herself over the second story balcony in a theatrical fit. She chuckled to herself at the thought, then verbally apologized to her aunt for the tenth time that day.

On Tate's second trip north, he was offered an auditing position in Virginia, Minnesota. It would take him an hour to drive to work each morning, but as he looked out at Shawaga Lake from the kitchen of their new house, he knew they had made the right decision. In that house they would make so many memories Tate had always wanted to instill into his children… Summers spent swimming and in metal fishing boats. Autumn nights drinking cider, watching the leaves turn red and orange in their backyard. Winter days spent laughing in the snow before warming their frozen bones beside a roaring fire in the family room.

"You're such a romantic," Joni often laughed at him. But he wanted so badly for these things to come true.

His wife had romantic notions of her own. As the house transformed, Joni felt her own schemes falling into place. She had spent the last twenty years fantasizing about a career in interior design, and Aunt Marie's house contained so many fulfilled promises and wishes within its very bones. She dreamed up business cards as she coated the walls white. She filled out tax forms and insurance claims as she shopped for furniture. After years of waiting, she would be a housewife no more.

Approximately five weeks and two days after Joni had received Mr. LeFoy's first phone call, the Harrison family loaded the last cardboard box into the moving truck, stepped into Tate's SUV, and began the journey to their new home.

CHAPTER THREE

Tate whistled as he stood in the foyer of their new house, looking at the walls and floors with open admiration.

"I've gotta admit… you really outdid yourself, honey," he murmured to his wife.

"Thank you," Joni beamed. She looked around as well. The antique wood floors remained the same, but all other traces of Aunt Marie had been stripped, lacquered or painted over. The foyer opened up to a wide expanse of living quarters with clean white walls and crisp modern furniture. Everything, from the black leather ottoman to the pendant light on the ceiling, felt contemporary and sophisticated. She had agonized over every purchase, over every picture frame and bauble. But as Joni stood in their new house, watching her family stare with open mouths, she knew that she had done a great job.

"I have my own room, don't I?" Avery asked, looking at her parents with a forlorn expression.

Joni got down on one knee and took her daughter's small pale hands in her own. Avery's teal sequined top shimmered in the sunlight that poured in from the large square windows that graced the front of the house. Her pink lips were scrunched as if in preparation for a pout.

"Avery, I know that you didn't want to move here. I know that it was hard for you to leave your school and your friends behind," Joni said in a soothing tone. Avery's mouth quivered as she nodded.

"Do you remember what I promised you the day we started packing up your room?"

Avery nodded slowly. "You said that I would love it here, and that you would give me a pink princess room like I've always wanted," she said.

"That's right," Joni murmured. "And I kept my promise. So why don't you go upstairs and find your new room?"

Avery's light brown eyes grew wide at her mother's words. With a high pitched squeal, she turned and raced to the staircase as quickly as her purple plastic flip-flops would allow. Joni turned to look at her husband with a satisfied smile, only to see him nervously gnawing at his bottom lip.

"Do I want to know how much that set us back?" he asked. His eyebrows inched toward his graying hairline.

"I promise it wasn't that much," Joni said, giving him a sympathetic pat on his back. "Most of the stuff came from IKEA, and I figured it would be worth it if it meant she wouldn't throw a tantrum every day that we are here."

A loud shriek of delight emanated from the ceiling above their heads, and they exchanged amused glances.

"Do I get a pink princess room too?" Adrian said from the doorway, readjusting the cardboard box he held with both hands.

Joni turned to her son with an exasperated expression. "Of course," she said, and began to laugh.

Over the course of the first week in the house, the Harrisons slowly unpacked their belongings and began to resume a sense of normalcy. Joni and Tate had timed the move so that their kids would have a week before they began classes at their new schools. It was spring break, and while the climate was much cooler than any of them had imagined, each of them silently enjoyed the reprieve from Florida's incessant humidity.

Tate started his new auditing job on their fourth day in the new house. When Joni asked him about it, he would always shrug good-naturedly. "Honey, auditing is about as interesting as watching grass grow," he smiled. "That's true no matter what state I'm in. The job is fine."

As Joni put the last of the frying pans and cups into the kitchen cupboards, she began to direct her attention to her own business. With Adrian's help, she began to design her own website where she would showcase her work. During most evenings she would wander aimlessly through the house, grinning as she eyed the thick white trim and the linen Roman shades. It would have sounded horrible to say, but secretly Joni believed her aunt's dying was one of the best things to ever happen to the Harrison family.

But of course not all of them could endure the transition so easily.

By the third night in the new house, Avery had seemingly already gotten used to the marvel that was her new bedroom. She looked at her vivid pink walls and white gauze canopy with unimpressed eyes and cried to her mother about her friends.

"You will make plenty of new ones at your new school, Av," Joni reassured her for what felt like the hundredth time. She tried to resist the temptation to grind her teeth together as her daughter followed her around the house, dramatically throwing herself onto the closest piece of furniture.

"I don't want new friends! I liked my old ones!" she yelled over and over again. The following Monday could not come swiftly enough.

Finally it had arrived. Joni kissed her daughter and watched as she disappeared behind her new teacher into the classroom, her head bent low in exaggerated despair. "For the love of all things holy, please make a friend, please make a friend," Joni whispered as she stared at the back of her daughter's head.

Luckily, the seven-year-old had taken after her father in terms of social prowess. Her voluminous array of hair bows and flashy sneakers indicated she had much to recommend her in the eyes of her fellow classmates, and by lunchtime she had made a handful of new friends.

She raved about all of them from the backseat of Joni's car that afternoon, and Joni smiled to herself, knowing she would never again hear about Avery's old friends in Florida.

Adrian had insisted on taking the bus on his first day at his new high school. Unlike his younger sister, he hadn't made any new friends. But also unlike his sister, he hadn't needed to. "I don't need friends if I know how to get to the library," he used to tell his parents. It had taken them several years to take his words to heart. To say Adrian was a recluse might have been an exaggeration, but there was no denying he was the least social of the family. Ben, an equally studious and closemouthed boy, had been the only person Joni and Tate saw Adrian hang out with on a steady basis. Every time they expressed concern, their son would laugh and wave them off with a flick of his hand. "I am my own friend," he'd smile knowingly.

Still, his junior year was drawing to a close, and Adrian privately fretted over his future. As he wandered from class to class, he didn't worry about friendships, but rather where he would go to college, and what sort of career he wanted. Being a solitary individual, he had cultivated many interests... none of which stood out among the rest.

These were the thoughts that occupied him as he sat down to dinner with his family a week and a half after moving into the new house. He shuffled peas around on his plate and said nothing.

"Adrian? You okay, sweetie?" Joni asked, her fork in midair as she frowned at her son across the table.

"I'm fine, just thinking," Adrian replied. He tried his best to put her mind at ease by smiling.

"Any cute girls in your classes?" Tate asked his son, and wiggled his eyebrows.

Adrian laughed and reached for his glass of water. "I think the real question is, are any of the girls in my classes cute AND intellectually stimulating—and that I can't answer yet," he replied.

Tate chuckled as he sawed his knife into a piece of steak. "Remind me again where we adopted him?" he asked, glancing at his wife.

Avery frowned as she watched her family laugh. "I don't get it," she complained, glaring at her half-empty plate.

"Don't worry about it, Av," Adrian told her. He leaned towards his sister in a conspiratorial manner. "Mom and Dad are just trying to be funny and are failing at it," he added in a mock whisper. Avery put a hand to her mouth as she giggled.

The family continued to eat in peaceful silence until Avery tossed one of her chicken nuggets back onto her plate and looked to her mother with sudden excitement. "Ooh, oh, I forgot to ask!" she exclaimed with wide eyes.

"Ask what?" Joni inquired.

"I was wondering if my friend Sarah could sleep over Friday night," Avery said, looking back and forth at her parents with hopeful glances.

"Who is Sarah?" Tate asked as he chewed.

"She's my new best friend!" Avery beamed. "She has curly blonde hair, and shoes that light up when she walks! Please, oh please, can she spend the night? She promised to bring over her princess Barbie dolls. She has Pocahontas and Ariel and everything!"

Joni and Tate exchanged silent, assessing glances over the white table. Social butterfly that Avery was, she had never asked for a friend to sleep over before. Tate made eye contact with his wife and gave a casual shrug.

"As long as I have a chance to speak with Sarah's mom beforehand… I don't see why not," Joni said.

Avery cried out in glee and practically bounced around in her seat. She smiled down at her plate as she finished her meal.

CHAPTER FOUR

The evening of Avery's first sleepover arrived. Joni had gone out of her way to make sure the event was truly a memorable one. While her daughter was still at school she had found the closest movie rental store and grabbed as many Disney princess movies as she could get her hands on. She had also spent an hour in the kitchen making funfetti cupcakes, complete with pink frosting.

From the moment Joni had picked her daughter up from school, Avery had been abuzz with agitated excitement. She raced around the first floor of their house, asking her mother over and over again if it was six o'clock yet.

"You're a big girl," Joni insisted. "You learned how to tell time back when you were in kindergarten. You tell me... is it six o'clock yet?"

Avery groaned, then stared up at the round analog clock Tate had nailed above the stove. "No, it isn't," she sighed.

"Well, I guess you have to wait, then," Joni said. She walked to the pantry and fished out a long sheet of plastic to cover the cupcakes with. Avery groaned and flung herself to the floor in frustration. Joni smiled to herself as she began to rinse out the large glass bowl she had used to mix the ingredients. She had acted much the same way in the hours leading up to her first sleepover as a little girl.

"Why don't you go upstairs and make sure that your dolls are all ready for the sleepover as well?" Joni suggested. Avery considered this and then bounded towards the stairs in a rush. She did not re-emerge until the doorbell rang two hours later.

"Oh, oh, oh!" Avery cried, practically flying down the wooden stairs. She had changed into a bright purple top and a rainbow hued tutu. Joni patiently waited as her daughter fumbled to unlock and open the front door.

Standing on the porch was a little girl, and a woman who was clearly her mother. Both had a shock of bright blonde curly hair that spiraled to their shoulders. The little girl bounced on the balls of her feet while her mother smiled kindly. Her eyes crinkled in the corners.

"Mrs. Harrison?" the woman asked, extending a hand.

"Hi!" Joni said, taking her hand in a friendly shake. "You must be Sarah's mom—sorry, Avery never supplied us with your last name."

"Crowder. But you can call me Jen," the blonde woman smiled.

"I'm Joni," Avery's mother said, tapping her chest. "And this beautiful young lady must be Sarah."

Sarah blushed and giggled, clearly delighted by the compliment. Joni waved them both inside. The four of them stood in the foyer as the two girls admired each other's outfits.

"Wow! I love your tutu," Sarah exclaimed, staring in admiration as Avery twirled in place.

"Thanks! I have a purple one you can borrow if you want," Avery said. "Do you want to put it on?"

"Yeah!" Sarah beamed.

The two girls had already begun to scramble up the steps before Mrs. Crowder called after her daughter. "I will pick you up at ten tomorrow morning, okay? If you need anything, just ask Mrs. Harrison to call me. I will leave my cell phone number with her, okay?"

"Okay," Sarah said, without bothering to glance back at her mom.

"I love you!" Mrs. Crowder said, but the two girls were already running up the steps, heedless of her words.

Jen's shoulders sank, but she smiled at Joni. "I wish I still had that boundless energy," she admitted.

Joni laughed. "Don't we all. Would you like something to drink? Perhaps a cup of coffee?"

Jen waved a hand in dismissal. "Thanks, but I have to get going. My husband has this work function we promised to attend. Total bore-fest, but you know the drill."

"My husband is an auditor, so yes, I understand—perhaps better than most."

Jen laughed and fidgeted with the lapel of her khaki trench coat. "Oh!" she said, and fished into her pocket. "Here is my cell number, along with my husband's. I should tell you that this is Sarah's first sleepover, so if she gets scared or nervous…"

Joni took the piece of paper with a kind smile. "I will make sure she knows she can call you whenever she needs to. This is Avery's first sleepover as well, though I'm sure it's much scarier being at someone else's house for the first time."

Jen nodded, but seemed at ease. "Sarah has done nothing but rave about Avery since the moment your daughter first arrived at school. I'm sure everything will be fine.

The two mothers exchanged a few more pleasantries before Jen said goodbye and disappeared down the driveway. Joni walked into the kitchen and placed the sheet of paper on the gray quartz countertop by the kitchen sink. She glanced at the clock before she made her way to the stairwell. A pizza would be arriving in about twenty minutes.

Joni walked down the carpeted hall until she got to Avery's room. Her daughter's door stood open, so she leaned into the doorframe and watched the two girls. They were already huddled on the floor in front of Avery's dollhouse, speaking in mock voices as they held dolls in their tiny fists. They didn't even notice that she was watching them.

"Sarah, do you like pizza?" Joni asked with a smile.

The blonde girl looked up from her doll and nodded enthusiastically.

"Great," Joni said. "Afterward, you guys can have cupcakes too."

The girls both cheered, then turned their attention back to their dolls. Joni meandered back down the hall and was about to walk downstairs when she felt compelled to check on Adrian.

His door was also open. Her son sat at his computer desk, absentmindedly drumming his fingers on its glass surface as he stared at the contents of a thick paperback book.

"What has you so preoccupied?" his mother asked from the doorway.

Silently, Adrian looked at her and then flipped the book closed so she could see its title. In large blue letters it read 'ACT TEST PREP.'

Joni cringed in sympathy. "God, I remember those days," she murmured. "I did so many practice tests I was about ready to rip my hair out."

Adrian chuckled appreciatively and pushed his toes against the tan carpet to face his mother. "Did you do well?" he asked.

Joni stepped into his room and smoothed a corner of his gray comforter so she could sit down on his twin bed.

"I think so," she nodded. "Not as well as your grandfather would have liked, but then nothing was ever good enough for your grandfather."

Adrian nodded, and ran a hand through his wavy black hair. His mother and grandfather had not had a good relationship when Grandpa Grezembski had been alive. Joni had never gone into much detail about it, but it always seemed that her father resented her for raising a family instead of pursuing a college degree.

"He'd be proud, you know," Joni murmured. "Seeing you prepare for that test. He always believed you'd make something of yourself," she smiled.

Adrian smiled back, but the expression did not reach his eyes. "But say I study until my eyes bleed," he murmured. "Say I study and study and I do well on the test, but have no idea what I want to do for a living. What then?"

Joni shrugged, but continued to smile at her son. "You apply to as many schools as you qualify for. After you get your acceptance letters—and you're bound to receive many—you see what schools offer the largest variety of degrees."

Adrian nodded as he fiddled with the edge of the prep book. "And then?" he asked.

"Then you choose a school and sign up for classes that sound interesting to you. Once you're taking classes every week you'll quickly realize what classes you love and what classes you hate. Over time you'll figure out what truly interests you. By your junior year of college, I bet you a million dollars you'll know what you want to do. And by then you'll be able to take courses strictly within that field."

Adrian nodded, but did not seem any more relaxed. He looked up at his mom. Joni stared into his eyes, the same hazel color as her own. "It's just so stressful," he sighed.

She leaned forward and gave his knee a sympathetic pat. "Honey, it's supposed to be. The fact that you are so stressed about it just shows me that you're taking your future seriously—as you should be."

"You're not worried that I have no idea what I want to do for a living?"

Joni shook her head and smiled. "I would only be worried if you were cavalier about the whole process. Adrian, you have the whole world at your feet. You're a brilliant young man... and I'm not just saying that because you're my offspring."

Adrian laughed. "Sure, because you're not biased or anything," he said, shaking his head.

"Of course not!" his mother cried, and laughed as well. She slowly got to her feet and ambled back to the door. The pizza would likely be arriving any minute.

"Mom?" Adrian called, still seated in his desk chair.

Joni looked back from the doorway. "Yeah?"

"You're a great mother," he said quietly, almost bashfully. "I think if Grandpa were still alive he would realize that, and he would be sorry for being so harsh on you when you were younger."

Joni felt her eyes grow wet as she looked at her son. "Thank you, sweetie," she whispered.

She fled down the hallway before the tears brimmed over onto her face. She wiped them away, still smiling over her son's words.

***

Fifteen minutes later Joni was hollering up the stairs, telling Avery and Sarah that the pizza was ready. The two girls bounded clumsily down the steps and appeared in the kitchen. Sarah wore Avery's bright purple tutu, and they had each brought a doll along.

"Belle is hungry," Avery informed her mother, wagging the doll in the air.

"Well, there's plenty enough to go around," Joni said, pointing to the paper plates she had placed on the table. The girls scrambled into their chairs and began to eat. The slices were so wide and flat the girls needed both hands to hold their pizza up to their mouths.

Adrian arrived minutes later, immediately followed by Tate, who grumbled under his breath and wiped oil from his hands onto a dirty cloth he retrieved from his back pocket.

"Have you figured out what's wrong?" Joni asked her husband as he walked to the sink and proceeded to wash his hands.

"No," Tate grumbled, shaking the excess water from his hands. "And I have half a mind to just give up and take it to a mechanic at this point, overcharges be damned."

Tate walked over to the table and sat down beside his son with a groan. Both of them opened the large cardboard box that sat at the center of the table, grabbed two slices and plopped them onto the paper plates Joni had laid out for them.

Joni walked to their stainless steel fridge and grabbed a beer. Returning to the kitchen table, she put it down in front of her husband before she took the vacant seat at the head of the table.

"Thank you," Tate said, flashing a grateful smile towards his wife as he chewed.

"Can I have one of those?" Adrian asked his mother, pointing toward the beer.

"No," Joni said, her tone flat. "But you're welcome to ask me again in a year."

Tate swallowed a mouthful of pizza before he turned his attention to Sarah, who was sitting quietly across from him. Her blue eyes had darted around to each of them as they had spoken.

"Sarah, that is a very becoming tutu you have on there," Tate said in a loud, jovial voice. "Both of you look like princesses!"

Sarah and Avery both giggled and continued to munch on their pizza.

"I heard this is your first sleepover," Tate said.

Sarah nodded, blushing from the roots of her blonde hair.

"Well, don't you worry, nobody in this family bites… much," he added as he leaned forward.

Sarah giggled again and beamed at Avery's father.

"Did you girls want to watch the movies I got you after you finish your pizza?" Joni asked. "I got *Frozen* and *Tangled*. You guys can even bring your sleeping bags down into the family room and sleep there if you wish."

"I can help you guys build a fort if you want, Av," Adrian added, nodding toward his sister.

"Oh, yes, please!" his little sister cried. She turned towards her friend. "My brother makes the best forts ever, and they never ever fall down."

"Cool!" Sarah said, and took another bite of her pizza.

For the next two hours Adrian helped his sister and Sarah construct an elaborate fort in their family room. Joni had grabbed all of the spare sheets out of the linen closet, as well as a handful of old clothespins. "Go ahead and take the kitchen chairs if you want," she had told him.

Joni listened to the girls' giggles as she wiped down the counters in the kitchen. "One more room!" they cried each time Adrian began to say the fort was just about finished. By the time they had run out of chairs and spare sheets, the fort took up over two thirds of the family room.

Joni laughed as she stared at the television and DVD player on the opposite side of the fort. "Well, your brother certainly did a good job," she told Avery. "Too good. I'm not sure how I'm going to be able to start a movie for you."

"I can do it!" Avery volunteered, holding her hands out for the DVD case.

Adrian's head emerged from the center of the fort. "I'm still here. Toss it to me, Mom, and I can crawl over to the TV."

"But I want to do it!" his sister said, stomping her foot. She folded her arms and scowled at her brother's head.

Joni and Adrian exchanged exasperated glances. Ever since they had moved, Avery had been insisting on doing many things by herself.

"Meet me by the TV, Av," Adrian called to her. "I'll show you how to do it, and when the first movie is over, you can put the second one in all by yourself. How about that?"

Avery thought this over for a moment before she gave her brother a brisk nod and disappeared into the labyrinth of blankets. Joni mouthed 'thank you' to her son and made her way back into the kitchen. She gingerly removed the plastic wrapping from the cupcakes she had made and placed two of them onto a clean paper plate.

The girls had finished *Tangled* and were halfway through *Frozen* before they finally fell asleep, their heads barely poking out of the edge of the fort, facing the television. Joni leaned over to check on them. Avery had a smudge of pink frosting on her nose, and Sarah clutched a Barbie doll to her chest while she slept.

Joni carefully bent at her waist to turn the TV off without knocking into the fort. She had kept the kitchen light on at a low setting in case either of the girls needed to get up and use the bathroom in the middle of the night.

Quietly she walked to the staircase and made her way up the steps. She heard the tell-tale sounds of a video game being played in Adrian's room. She stopped and listened by his door and considered poking her head in to say goodnight. She hovered there for a moment and then shook her head and continued down the hall. She didn't want to break his concentration. Her poor son had spent hours studying that day. He deserved a well-earned break.

She made her way into her and Tate's room. Her husband was a lump under the duvet. He was snoring softly and didn't budge when she closed the door behind her. With a silent yawn, Joni crept under the covers and scooted her body close to her husband's. Tate mumbled incoherently in his sleep, but wrapped his arm around her out of habit. Joni closed her eyes and was asleep within minutes.

When she woke again, the room was still bathed in darkness. She blinked and wondered what had woken her. She peered into the darkness and flinched when she saw the faintest silhouette of a human shape standing at her side of the bed.

"What the…?" she mumbled.

The shadow moved as she spoke, and slowly began to cry. "Mrs. Harrison?" a timid voice said in the dark.

"Sarah?" Joni said, sitting up in bed. She furiously rubbed at her eyes, trying to clear the last remnants of her dream from her mind.

The shadow cried harder at the sound of her own name. Joni threw the duvet back and lowered her feet until she felt the carpet below. She stood up and quietly guided Sarah to the bedroom door, which she had left open a crack.

When they got into the hallway, Joni closed the bedroom door behind her, then fumbled for the light switch. Harsh yellow light flooded the hall, and Joni blinked several times before the blonde girl came into focus beside her.

Sarah continued to cry as she half covered her eyes with her hands. Swearing internally, Joni lowered herself to her knees so she was eye level with the blonde girl.

"Shh… shh, it's okay, Sarah, it's okay. I'm here."

Sarah flung her arms around Joni and clung to her, crying with renewed energy. Joni rubbed the back of the girl's purple nightgown, making soothing sounds with her throat.

After several minutes Sarah seemed to calm down enough to speak. Joni carefully pried her away so she could look into the little girl's face. "What's wrong, Sarah? Did you have a bad dream?"

Sarah shook her head from side to side, her blonde hair bouncing back and forth.

"I'm scared," she whispered. She looked into Joni's eyes with an expression of sheer terror.

Joni nodded and pulled a tear-streaked strand of blonde hair away from the girl's face. "It's okay, I'm here. What are you scared of?"

Sarah opened her mouth, then closed it again, as if unsure of what to say. She stared helplessly at Joni and looked as though she would start crying all over again.

"It's okay. Nothing is going to hurt you. I am right here," Joni reassured her—if only to keep the girl from another round of tears.

Sarah nodded silently and hiccupped. She murmured something under her breath and hiccupped again.

"What did you say, sweetie?" Joni asked, leaning closer to the girl's face so she could hear.

"The thing," Sarah whispered, and shuddered visibly.

Joni frowned and took a deep breath, trying her best to be patient. "The thing?" she repeated.

Sarah nodded with wide eyes. She clutched Joni's shoulders as if at any moment the woman would stand up and leave her alone in the hallway.

"What thing?" Joni asked her.

"The dark thing," Sarah whispered, and erupted into tears all over again.

Joni drew in a deep breath and held Sarah against her chest. She rubbed the little girl's back as she sobbed into Joni's shoulder.

The whole evening had gone so well that Joni had convinced herself that Avery and her friend were old enough to handle a sleepover. Unfortunately, she had been wrong. It was abundantly clear that Sarah was not yet ready to be away from her parents for an entire night. And that likely meant that Avery wasn't quite ready either.

Joni held Sarah in her arms until the girl quieted down. "Would you like to go home, Sarah?" she asked the little girl. She felt Sarah nod her head into her shoulder.

"Alright," Joni said. She placed her hands on Sarah's shoulders and pulled her away from her shoulder once more. She rose to her full height but held her hand out to Sarah. The blonde girl took it with shaky fingers.

"Your mom left her phone number with me just in case you needed her. Let's go downstairs and call her, okay?"

Sarah began to cry and shake her head the moment the word 'downstairs' left Joni's lips.

"It's okay, it's okay, I am going with you," the woman insisted. She stared into Sarah's wide blue eyes to show her she was serious. "I will be with you the entire time. You can hold my hand just like this until your mom comes to pick you up, okay, honey?"

Sarah gulped in air. She nodded and gripped Joni's hand more securely with her fingers. The pair of them slowly made their way down the stairs and into the kitchen. Sarah kept jerking her head around as if she were looking for someone or something. With her free hand Joni flipped on the kitchen light. She could tell by the quiet family room that Avery was still fast asleep inside the fort.

Still holding Sarah's hand, Joni walked to the counter where she had placed Mrs. Crowder's phone number. She picked it up and walked to the white plastic phone on the wall.

"Sarah, I'm going to call your mom now, okay? But in order to do so, I need my hand. Is that alright?"

"Nooo!" Sarah cried out, clutching at Joni's hand as if her life depended on it.

"I've got to," Joni insisted. "It's the only way I can dial the number, sweetie. I'm not going anywhere, I promise."

Sarah gave one last tearful sob before she slowly let go of Joni's hand. The woman flexed her fingers before she looked at the piece of paper and punched in the numbers with her freed hand.

The phone rang several times before she heard a sleepy "Hello?" on the other end.

"Mrs. Crowder? Hi, it's Mrs. Harrison," Joni murmured into the phone, hoping Avery wouldn't wake up in the next room.

"Mrs. Harrison?" the voice repeated, puzzled.

"Avery's mom," Joni said. "I'm so sorry to call you in the middle of the night, but Sarah is pretty upset and would like to go home." She stared down at Sarah as the girl continued to jerk her head all around, as if searching for something.

"I don't think she was ready for a sleepover after all," Joni said in an even quieter voice.

"Sarah?" Mrs. Crowder said. She seemed to wake up a bit more at the sound of her daughter's name.

"Yes," Joni said and stifled a yawn. "She wants you to come get her."

Mrs. Crowder took a deep breath and murmured, "Okay, I will be there in ten minutes," before she hung up the phone.

When Mrs. Crowder's headlights lit up the house, she saw Joni and her daughter sitting on the front porch, hunched over against the cold.

"What are you guys doing out in the cold?!?" Jen asked as she made her way to the front of the house. She looked at Joni as if the woman were crazy.

Joni shrugged apologetically. "Sarah insisted on going outside. She didn't stop crying until we were out here."

Mrs. Crowder scowled at her but said nothing. Silently, she reached out for her daughter. Sarah practically leapt into her mother's arms and began to cry all over again. "Mommy," she blubbered.

Joni reached behind her and grabbed the bag Jen had packed for her overnight stay. "I'm sorry," she said, and handed the pack over, unsure of what else to say.

Jen nodded. Her scowl lessened slightly when she saw how sincere Joni was. "Me too," she said. "Get in the car, Sarah."

Sarah let go of her mother and ran to the dark blue car as if something was chasing her there. The two mothers exchanged awkward glances before Jen turned without a word and marched back to her vehicle.

Joni stood in the freezing cold air and watched as Jen turned around in the driveway and made her way down the long dirt road that ran parallel to the lake. She watched the red taillights grow smaller and smaller until they turned and disappeared into the darkness.

She shivered and hastened to the front door of the house. She slowly pulled it open and then closed it softly behind her. She walked through the foyer and poked her head into the family room. The dim light from the kitchen was still on and she could see that her daughter was still fast asleep inside the fort.

Joni stared down at Avery, unsure of what to do. She didn't want her daughter to wake up the following morning and discover that her friend was gone. Even worse, she didn't want Avery to wake up and find herself all alone in the dark family room. And yet if she did wake her and carry her to her bed, Avery would realize that Sarah was missing and would likely begin to cry.

No matter what, Joni knew that her daughter would wind up in tears. She stifled another yawn. She was too exhausted to make any decision, really. With a sigh, Joni got down on her hands and knees and crawled into the fort. She stretched her body out beside her daughter's and wiggled experimentally against the coarse carpet. She knew that her body would punish her for spending the night on the hard floor, but she also knew it was the best solution.

She shifted and sighed and dreaded the fit she knew the morning would inevitably bring.

CHAPTER FIVE

Six hours later, Avery shook her mother awake, her small hands on either side of her mother's shoulders.

"Mommy? Mommy, wake up! Sarah is gone!" Avery cried. Joni could hear the panic in her voice.

She groaned and slowly sat up. Her head touched the top of the fort. She blinked and looked at her daughter, who still hovered over her, a wrinkle between her eyebrows.

"Where's Sarah?" Avery demanded.

"Honey, Sarah got scared in the middle of the night. I called her mom and Sarah went home. I didn't want to wake you up. I'm sorry."

Joni grimaced as her daughter let loose a high pitched wail. Avery crawled out of the fort, ignoring her mother as she called after her. Sobbing, the seven-year-old ran up the steps and down the hallway. Joni could hear her bedroom door slam shut.

"Shit," Joni muttered to herself. She slowly crawled out of the fort. Several of her vertebrae cracked as she stood up and shuffled into the kitchen. Every part of her body ached in protest. Slowly, she lowered her body into a chair at the table. She looked at the other side of the kitchen where the black Keurig sat on the counter. She desperately wanted coffee, but her body hurt too much to move again.

With a groan, Joni lowered her head against the cool white table and decided she would lie there for all eternity.

She must have dozed off, because when she opened her eyes again, Adrian was standing over her with a look of concern on his face.

"Mom? You okay?" he asked, scanning her face with his eyes.

"No. Please shoot me," Joni groaned and slowly raised her head. Now her neck ached as well.

"What's wrong?" Adrian asked, taking a seat beside her.

"Sarah crept into my room last night and woke me up sobbing," Joni said. "She was scared and wanted to go home, so I called her mom and waited until Mrs. Crowder showed up. I didn't want your sister to wake up in the family room alone, so I crawled into the tent and slept next to her for the rest of the night."

"Ah." Adrian nodded. "Well, that explains why Avery is sobbing in her room right now."

"Yes," Joni replied flatly. "Honey, will you please make me a cup of coffee? My body hates me right now."

Adrian chuckled, but stood up and walked to the Keurig. He opened a cupboard and pulled out a mug, which he set onto the stand of the machine. He punched a button with his index finger. The gurgling sound of the machine was music to Joni's ears. He walked back to his mother and placed a steaming mug of coffee in front of her.

"Bless you," she murmured, and took a long sip.

"What was Sarah so frightened of?" Adrian asked, sitting back down beside his mother.

Joni raised one hand, still holding her cup of coffee with the other. "I have no idea," she said, shaking her head. "I remember her muttering about 'the thing' a couple of times, but I couldn't make heads or tails of it. She probably had a nightmare. I don't think she was quite ready to spend the night at someone else's house."

Adrian frowned down at the kitchen table. "That's weird… I mean, I know they're young and everything, but she seemed just fine when they were eating and watching the movies last night. It doesn't make sense."

Joni shrugged her shoulders and took another sip of coffee. "Beats me," she murmured. "All I know is that your sister is probably going to pout about it for the rest of the weekend."

"Probably," Adrian said with a look of sympathy.

Sure enough, Avery scowled, cried and complained for the remainder of the weekend. Multiple times, Joni tried to explain to her that Sarah had been scared—that it hadn't been Avery that she was trying to get away from. Each time Avery would just wail and run back to her room, slamming the door behind her. Joni tried her best to be patient. She knew that the moment school started up again the following Monday, all would be forgotten.

Unfortunately, that wasn't true. When Avery sat down beside Sarah in the cafeteria, the blonde girl refused to speak with her. Confused, Avery asked her what was wrong, but the blonde girl just sniffed in response, grabbed her tray and moved to a different table. One by one, the other girls around them followed suit. Joni was shocked when she arrived at the elementary school four hours later to find her daughter's face streaked with tears.

"Nobody will talk to me!" Avery sobbed when Joni asked her what was wrong.

In the week that followed, Joni, Tate and Adrian made it a point to be extra nice to Avery. Joni packed an extra cookie in her lunch each day. Tate would give her extra hugs when he arrived home from work each evening. And Adrian let Avery hang out in his room while he did homework. As the days progressed, Avery slowly returned to her usual chipper self. She started to talk about a new group of friends from school. Never again did she mention Sarah or the night of their sleepover.

Until one Saturday morning, three weeks later. The family were all seated at the kitchen table, enjoying breakfast. Joni had made eggs and bacon while Tate had made a pile of pancakes on the stovetop. Everything seemed normal and pleasant until a natural lull occurred in the conversation and Avery turned to look at her parents.

"Mom? Dad?"

"Yeah?" Tate replied as he slathered a pad of butter onto his pancakes.

"Do you think you could get rid of the thing that lives under the staircase?" Avery asked.

Joni and Tate looked at each other, puzzled by her question.

"The thing that lives under the stairs?" Joni repeated, staring at her daughter uncertainly.

Avery nodded and stabbed at her pile of eggs. "It keeps pinching my feet when I go down the stairs at night."

Tate swallowed a mouthful of pancakes and slowly set his fork and knife down upon the table. "What are you talking about, Av?" he asked.

Avery snorted with impatience. "I just told you," she complained mildly. "The black thing. You know? It lives under the staircase. It likes to pinch my feet when I walk down the stairs after dark."

Joni blinked and continued to stare at her daughter. "The black thing…" she repeated.

Avery nodded and stabbed at her pile of scrambled eggs again. "Yeah," she said. "I think I made it mad."

"Made it mad?" Adrian said. He was also staring at Avery, a look of slight concern on his face.

She nodded matter-of-factly. "A couple of weeks ago it asked me if I wanted to play. I asked what it wanted to do. The thing said that it wanted to play in the basement. But I don't like the basement," Avery said. "It's dark and creepy down there—and that's what I told the black thing.

But it kept saying it wanted to play in the basement. So I said that I wouldn't play with it."

Avery glanced at each of her family members as they continued to stare at her, confused looks plastered on their faces.

"I think I made it mad after that," she added quietly. "Now every time I walk down the stairs, it reaches out and pinches my feet. Could you please tell it to stop? Because the pinches really hurt."

Joni looked to her husband, who glanced back at her, a cup of orange juice poised at his lips. When Adrian was a child, he had always been inquisitive about everything. It felt like Joni and Tate had personally kept the shelves of the neighborhood grocery store bare of child-proofing mechanisms. There was no drawer, box, container, cupboard or toilet in their house that did not have some lock or puzzle attached. Even so, Joni and Tate felt they had met their match in terms of mechanical ingenuity.

When Avery began to transition from toddlerhood to girlhood, she was an emotional rollercoaster. There was no topic out of bounds when it came to talking to her, and her reactions were often dramatic and theatrical in nature. From their second child, Joni and Tate had learned how best to communicate with a child.

However, in all of their experience, not once had their kids ever mentioned an imaginary character before. Not an imaginary friend... not even an imaginary monster in the closet.

Joni glanced from her husband to her daughter with thinly veiled uncertainty. "Sweetie, are you talking about someone invisible?" she asked, attempting to sound casual. She fidgeted with a piece of toast on her plate.

Avery waved her small pink fork in the air with a brisk 'no.'

She grabbed a piece of bacon and bit at it with exaggerated force. After she had chewed and swallowed, she leaned over the table with a serious expression on her face.

"It's not invisible, and you better be quieter, or it will hear you. It lives under the stairs."

She glanced at her brother, who made eye contact with her. He had barely touched the array of food on his plate.

"If it asks you to play with it, don't go. It's mean," she whispered to Adrian.

Adrian frowned, but nevertheless nodded. It was clear that Avery took what she was saying very seriously. He didn't want to hurt her feelings by appearing amused.

Still, it was unlike his sister to suddenly fib about inconsequential things. Adrian absentmindedly poked a fork into his eggs, wondering if Sarah's cold shoulder was having a more negative impact on Avery than any of them had thought.

Meanwhile, Joni was pouring a packet of sugar into her coffee as she attempted to reason with her daughter.

"You were probably just having a dream," she said. She picked up a small silver spoon and stirred the contents of her pale yellow coffee cup.

Avery shook her head, looking strangely smug. It wasn't often she had news before her parents did. It made her feel she had some semblance of power. "It wasn't a dream," she replied. "It happened again and again, and I was awake every time."

Tate nibbled on a triangular piece of toast and considered his daughter as he chewed. Joni rose from the table and glided to one of the gray cabinets for some Tupperware. "Well, you said you refused to play with it, right?" she asked as she came back to the table.

Avery briefly considered the question before she nodded her head and took another chunk out of her bacon.

"Well, you probably hurt its feelings," Joni reasoned. She grabbed the plate of bacon and slid the leftovers into the plastic storage container. "Perhaps next time you should play with it. It probably wouldn't pinch you then."

Tate chuckled at his wife's joking response. Avery, however, proceeded to pout and climbed down from the table in a frustrated huff.

The three remaining Harrisons listened for the inevitable sounds of Avery stomping up the stairs and then the slam of her door being forced closed.

"I should probably get one of those slow-closing mechanisms for that door," Tate said to his wife, looking apologetic.

"Probably a good idea," Joni replied, and winced as she touched her neck.

CHAPTER SIX

Life, for a brief while anyway, resumed as normal. Avery reached out to girls in other classes and slowly but surely made a steady group of solid friends. Tate continued to acclimate himself to the inner politics of his new office. Joni worked on her website and attempted to land her first client. Adrian continued to wonder what type of career would make him happy.

The Harrisons got used to their new life in their new house, sometimes referring to it as Lakeside, like everyone else did. And the house, in turn, got used to them. It grew familiar with their day-to-day ablutions and habits. Tate enjoyed listening to classic rock at max volume as he tinkered with his BMW in the garage. The bass reverberated through the structure of the house, rippling out in steady waves.

Joni and Avery both enjoyed extensive singing in the shower. The acoustics of the cream tiled room made each of them sound five times better than they actually were. And Adrian had nurtured an unusual habit since the time he turned eleven. Whenever he felt as though he were in the middle of some sort of dilemma, he dealt with it by rearranging the furniture in his room. Something about the heavy, mindless labor of it helped put his thoughts at ease. It was strange at first, the sounds of furniture being moved around on a routine basis. When Marie had lived in the house, nothing had ever budged from its dust-covered place. To the house, it was a most peculiar behavior.

With each passing week, the family grew more accustomed to the varying noises the house made at night—all save for Joni. She often found herself blissfully unaware of the houses creaks and moans during the day, but at night everything was different. All was quiet save for this most peculiar scraping noise that emanated from the hall.

Joni sighed as she rolled onto her side, casting the pillow down over her head as if to block the noise. Their thick cream comforter lay in a pitiful, twisted heap at her feet, and she would occasionally kick it in equal parts frustration and exhaustion. She turned her head to the left to peek at her sleeping husband sprawled out on the other half of the bed. His nose whistled softly as he slept. She marveled at his ability to remain asleep despite her persistent thrashing.

Studying Tate's tousled black hair made Joni's eyes grow heavy with contentment. She felt herself slowly sinking into the mattress, on the brink of sleep, when another long scraping sound came from the hall.

"Adrian," Joni half whispered out loud. He had been a little anxious of late, feeling the magnitude of his impending graduation from high school. Joni had remembered reaching that very point when she was a junior like her son. It was as if she woke up one day and the weight of the world was suddenly on her shoulders. She needed to decide her destiny. The dilemma had caused her many restless nights of pacing in her bedroom. She could not begrudge Adrian his coping mechanism for enduring the necessary transition into adulthood.

Even at the expense of her precious sleep.

With a soft groan, Joni reached forward on the bed, grabbing her comforter with pinched fingers. She pulled the heavy blanket over her head and tossed the pillow on top, as if to cradle her head. She could still hear the scraping noises, but they were muffled and distant. Joni smiled and closed her eyes, certain she had found the trick.

The following morning Adrian had his nose deep within a book. Joni glanced at the cover as she set a pitcher of orange juice down on the white kitchen table. AP-PLIED PHYSICS, it read in tall, bold letters. An array of formulas in a myriad of colors were set in a stripe pattern underneath the title. Joni watched her son's eyes as they sped back and forth across the page, a frown disappearing and reappearing across his brow.

She decided she would not make any comments about his late-night rearranging. She knew he would feel unnecessarily guilty.

But when Adrian decided to move things around for the second night in a row, Joni tossed aside her pillows and clambered out of bed. She was too exhausted to handle it with grace. With draggy feet, she meandered down the hall and arrived in front of Adrian's door.

She expected the door to be closed, but found it open a small gap. Joni took a step forward, careful to step over a weak spot in the wood floor where it creaked incessantly. She peered through the gap in the door and blinked in confusion.

Joni expected to see Adrian leaning up against his dresser, grunting with the effort of pushing it across the floor. She expected to see his light on and the television blaring as he reconfigured the contents of his room.

Instead, there was nothing but darkness. From the faint moonlight that swept into the room from the window, Joni could see the outline of her son, sleeping on his side between his plaid sheets. Adrian's chest of drawers, bookcases and desk were all in the exact same places they had been since they first moved in, weeks prior.

Puzzled, Joni let her eyes wander around the various books and knick-knacks of her son's room as she attempted to be logical. She had been so certain the noise was caused by Adrian. What else could it have been?

As if on cue, the loud scratching noise began again. Joni slowly turned in place, pressing her ear to the wall of the hallway. She felt the vibrations ripple out from somewhere down the hall.

With bare feet, Joni tiptoed down the hallway towards the wooden staircase. It sounded as if the noise was coming from inside the wall, to the immediate left of the landing. Joni pressed her face against the wall again and listened. A dull light poured into the elongated hall from a small circular window at the top of the stairwell. Shadows were cast down the hall into long, distorted shapes. Joni stood at the top of the landing and tried to look down onto the floor below. The staircase, which was ancient, despite a fresh coat of white paint, turned sideways and into the shadows. Joni found herself staring, wondering if at any moment someone would appear on the platform to glance up at her.

She shuddered and turned her attention back to the hallway. The lack of light was giving her the creeps. "Get a grip," she told herself, and walked back towards her and Tate's bedroom.

Joni lay back down again, but it was several hours later when she finally fell asleep. She spent the time in between staring at the dead branches of the tree outside the window, listening as the scratching persisted through-out the night.

In the morning she was irritable and short with every-one. Avery began to cry, but was immediately distracted by a crooked stack of pancakes her father placed on the table in front of her. Adrian sat at the far end of the table, listening to his parents talk while pretending to read *The Hobbit*.

"I'm telling you, babe, there's something there, and I am losing my beauty sleep because of it," Joni muttered. She jabbed at link sausages that sizzled on the skillet in front of her. Circles, deep purple in hue, were visible on her cheeks even from a short distance.

Tate looked at his wife as he shimmied a pile of pancakes onto a plate on the gray quartz counter. "What do you think it is?" he asked.

Joni shrugged her shoulders under her terry cloth bathrobe. "Maybe a bird, or a mouse that has gotten stuck between the walls. Maybe even old piping? I really don't know."

Tate pinched his lips together, but nodded good naturedly. His wife wasn't prone to exaggeration. "Alright," he said. "I will contact someone, get them to come out and check on the foundation of the house and such."

Joni flashed her husband a grateful smile before flipping the switch on the stove off. "Thank you," she said, before carrying the food to the kitchen table.

CHAPTER SEVEN

Two days later, Tate was escorting a rigid looking older man across the stone pathway that led to the front of the house. The man had thin strands of graying hair stuck to his wrinkled skull. He walked as though his knees wouldn't bend.

"None of the rest of us have heard it, but my wife says it happens late at night, somewhere along the second story," Tate was saying as he hovered near the man. They had made it to the wide front porch when Tate extended his hand, clutching onto the crook of the older man's elbow.

"Let me help you, Mr. Lindstrom," he said with an open smile. He grabbed the brown leather satchel the man was carrying and took the weight into his own hands.

Mr. Lindstrom grunted a 'thank you' in return. "My legs don't cooperate like they used to," he said, his voice feeble yet humorous.

The two gentlemen slowly made it across the threshold, and into the foyer of the house. The house was still and quiet. Tate looked at the scattering of furniture in the den and the round potted plant beside the door and found himself smiling. It wasn't often he was alone in the house and was able to take a step back and appreciate the backdrop that made up their new life.

Tate shook his head and looked to find Mr. Lindstrom standing next to him beside the door, waiting for Tate to take the lead once more.

"Oh, right, well, the noise is coming from up here," he said, pointing to their immediate left, where the white painted staircase curved up onto the second floor landing.

Mr. Lindstrom stared at the stairs and gave a brisk nod. He took a deep breath, and the pair slowly worked their way up the stairs. As Tate helped the older man keep his balance, he glanced down at the small white steps beneath his gym socks. The treads met tightly with the risers of the next step, leaving no gap in between. Why had Avery insisted that something was pinching her when nothing could go through the staircase?

Kids, Tate thought with an amused sigh.

After what felt like an hour, Mr. Lindstrom was safely up the staircase, and was staring at the wall in question. His yellowed eyes flitted from the wall to the ceiling and back again. He muttered to himself through thin, pale lips.

With a shaky hand, he pointed to the bag Tate still held.

"Oh," Tate said, and opened the worn flap. Inside were large rectangular papers with structural designs on them. As Tate rifled through them he realized they were blueprints. His eyes scanned each page until one set looked familiar. Gingerly he pulled them from the bag and offered them to Mr. Lindstrom.

The older man continued to mutter under his breath as he leafed through the prints. Finally, he found what he was looking for and held it up against the robin's egg blue wall of the hallway. He slowly began to shake his head.

"No... There aren't any pipes that are running through this wall. If I were you, I would check with a structural engineer and then an exterminator," Mr. Lindstrom said as he slid the blueprints back into his satchel.

Tate's shoulders sunk, but his face lacked surprise. He'd figured that was what the plumber would say. Both the upstairs and downstairs toilets ran along the other side of the house. It wouldn't make any sense that Joni would be hearing the pipes.

Tate was courteous as he waved Mr. Lindstrom good-bye as the older man got into his dented old pickup truck and sputtered his way down the driveway.

Next came a structural engineer. Thankfully, this gentleman was much younger. Tate and Joni followed him around the house like lost lambs. The engineer, who enthusiastically introduced himself as Kent, spent the next hour scrunching up the bridge of his nose to keep his large silver glasses in place as he peered up into the attic, down into the depths of the cement basement, and into every nook and cranny of the closets.

Afterward, Tate, Joni and Kent reconvened in the kitchen. The trio sat down at the rectangular kitchen table, each clutching a steaming cup of coffee in their palms.

"First of all, I just want to commend you for having the house inspected. It's historic, and that usually means a lot of wear and tear," Kent pontificated as he stirred a touch of cream into his coffee.

Joni snuck an amused look at her husband before leaning onto the table. "So, you mean there is a problem? Structurally, I mean?"

Kent raised his eyebrows into his shaggy brown hair. "Actually, no. You said this house was owned by your aunt, right? Well, she did a great job with the upkeep. Everything looks up to date and up to code."

He pursed his lips to sip delicately at his coffee before placing it back down on the table. Tate wondered if the man's exaggerated theatrics were simply because this was likely the most interesting thing on his schedule that day. Strange noises, terrified, attractive woman… There were a number of B movies that started that way, weren't there?

"I don't know what is causing the disturbance," Kent whispered, boring his eyes into Joni's. "But at this point, I think it's safe to say that it's supernatural… or, you have an infestation of some kind."

The couple thanked Kent profusely, then immediately began to laugh the moment the door was closed.

Next came the exterminator—a far less amusing visit in Joni's eyes. She was generally against anything that slithered or crawled or could lay eggs in your ear canal. The very idea made her shiver.

"It won't be a big deal." Tate ran a hand through her hair as they waited, attempting to comfort her.

Joni looked up at her husband with disbelief. "Won't be a big deal? The idea that at this very moment there are a thousand bugs crawling around eating our walls? Oh, it makes me sick," she squealed, and shuddered again, to which Tate laughed.

Russell, the exterminator, was a fairly chatty fellow, and looked to be somewhere between Mr. Lindstrom and Kent in age. His dark brown eyes were magnified in his bifocal glasses, but he seemed friendly and his wit was sharp.

"Yes, none of the ladies like it when I visit," Russell said. He made a tutting sound with his teeth. "Too busy imagining me covered in creepy crawlies, I suspect," he added with a knowing smile at Joni.

Donning a bright orange jumpsuit, the man marched around the house much like Kent the engineer had. He sprayed chemicals on the walls, examined minuscule particles of debris on the floor, and used tiny, almost wire-thin cameras to peer into the floor boards.

Russell and Tate circled back from the backyard to the front of the house, where Joni stood hunched on the front porch, pulling weeds out of a hanging fern.

"Well, Mrs. Harrison, I'm happy to report that your house is vermin-free," Russell smiled, his fists on his hips.

"Really?" Joni asked. She anxiously fidgeted with the brown weed in her hands. Tate noticed the subtle gesture and briefly frowned at his wife.

"Really," Russell smiled. "You can sleep peacefully. Have a good day, folks."

"Take care," Tate called after him before turning to face his wife. The planked wooden porch groaned slightly under his weight.

Tate reached out and took his wife's free hand, intertwining her slender fingers with his stubby, hairy ones. "You don't look relieved. Why is that?" he asked quietly, staring into her green hued eyes.

Joni shrugged and stared down at her husband's worn Led Zeppelin t-shirt. "It's true that I wouldn't be happy knowing our new house is full of rodents or bugs," she murmured. "But that also means that we still have no idea where the noise is coming from."

With a small smile, Tate grabbed the ends of Joni's teal colored sweater and led her down the white porch steps onto the sloping lawn in front of their house. He planted her right in the middle of their lawn, then slowly bent down to kiss her forehead before spinning her around to face the house.

Tate shifted his legs and stood, at ease, beside her. "Now then," he said in a mock serious tone. "Look up at our house. Tell me what you see."

"Um," Joni giggled in hesitation, staring at her husband, who was trying not to smile. When he looked at her questioningly, she shook her head and complied.

The front of the house had so many windows and ornate details that it was hard to focus on just one thing at first. It had been the only part of the house Aunt Marie had truly neglected. When Joni first arrived in Minnesota, the house had chipped paint and a couple of wooden shutters that were halfway off their hinges.

Like much of her house, Marie had painted the outside a rich plum color. Joni was sure the color was beautiful, at the right time of year. But combined with the uneven paver stones, and the overgrown shrubbery, the house gave the overall appearance of being abandoned.

When she had pictured finally starting her interior design business, she had pictured the house in a wash of white with crisp black shutters. Joni had dismantled the house piece by piece until it felt modern and brand new.

Still… under all the fresh coats of paint, behind all the new light fixtures, behind the very walls, there was still the undeniable truth: it was a very old house.

Joni sighed, knowing that this was the answer Tate was looking for.

"Warped wood, scratched windows… it looks tired," she admitted.

"Yes," her husband replied as he began to move his hands in a cycling motion. "And why would it look tired?"

"Because it's old."

"How old?"

"Very old," Joni muttered through gritted teeth—and yet she couldn't help but smile at his antics whenever he wasn't looking.

Tate snapped his fingers with satisfaction. "Aha! It's old… very old." His face relaxed, and he gently grabbed Joni by her shoulders. "It might not be pipes or rodents, but we no longer live in a modern ranch-style house in Deland. We are living in history now, my dear." He smiled and stroked her chin. "And history is never quiet."

Joni rolled her eyes, but smiled up at her husband, leaning into his touches. "Alright, you've made your point. I won't worry about the noises anymore."

She had meant to do well by that promise. Joni tried to sleep with the television on, so as to drown the noise. But nothing ever helped. Late into the night, the noise would begin and Joni's eyes would flip open as if she had been waiting for it all along.

CHAPTER EIGHT

Life resumed in the Harrison household. Despite the incessant scratching Joni heard at night, everything else appeared to be quite normal. While Tate and the kids were away at work and school, Joni would fiddle with her new design website. Each day she woke up she would throw back the long linen curtains in her and Tate's bedroom and tell herself that today would be the day she got her first client.

At first, Joni sat in front of the computer desk, staring at her email inbox, waiting for something to happen. Within a few days she began allowing herself to get up to wash a couple of wayward dishes in the sink and start a load of laundry or two.

By the second week, she had given up looking at her inbox entirely. Instead she took out all of her aggression on the grout of the main floor bathroom, or the mildew that had collected in the cracks of the tile floor of the kitchen. Anything that kept her from staring at the screen of her failures.

Thus, Joni fell back into old habits. Out came the vacuum and the extendable microfiber duster. As she scoured, poured, stirred and scrubbed, she felt her exhaustion and fear of failure drain from her fingertips into the scummy water of the mop bucket.

It was on a Thursday when things started to get a bit strange.

A storm hovered over the lake, and the horizon merged with the water until it was one dark hazy line. The wind whipped through the trees, causing them to sway down to their very roots. Rain pelted down onto the rear windows of the house, making a loud thudding noise that Joni found soothing as she stood in the family room, folding laundry.

She had tossed the basket on top of a black leather armchair and was using the adjacent matching couch to sort the clothes into piles. Joni tried her best to suppress her despair about her failed business, instead letting her thoughts wander about the house.

She stopped moving, halfway done folding one of Avery's sequin-infested shirts, when she looked up at the ceiling above her head. Everything, save for the distant ticking of the analog clock in the kitchen, was silent.

She frowned as she finished folding the shirt and tossed it onto the couch. It didn't quite add up. Each and every night she battled for sanity against the steady influx of scratching and thudding noises that came from somewhere in the hall. Since the house had passed its inspections, Tate had proposed that it was merely the house settling.

"Think about it," he had reassured her. "Every day it's getting colder, especially at night. The house contracts because of the temp, that's all." And he had kissed the center of her forehead.

But if the house contracted due to dropping temperatures at night, didn't that also imply it would expand again come morning?

How was the house eerily quiet by day, and an endless cacophony of noise at night?

Lost in thought, she reached into the plastic basket and felt something rough and solid with her fingers. Her frown deepened as she glanced into the basket. There, lying on top of one of Tate's pinstriped shirts and Adrian's black flannel, was a silver knife with a thick black handle.

With her thumb and index finger, Joni picked it up and held it up to her face. It was nothing fancy. It was just a standard steak knife, from a set she had purchased with a coupon from a wholesale grocer.

"How in the world did you end up in here?" Joni asked the knife. She held it out from her body as she walked to the kitchen, holding it the way children are instructed to handle scissors.

She crossed over the tile floor to the dishwasher. As she opened the latch and swung the door down, she imagined herself putting the knife into the cutlery drawer instead. It had been washed, hadn't it? She chuckled to herself and ambled back into the family room.

With ginger movements she felt around the remaining clothes in the basket. There weren't any more knives.

Nevertheless, they began to appear in the strangest of places.

Joni was vacuuming the family room a few days after the laundry incident. There was an unusual bounce of enthusiasm in her step, as she had received a request for a quote from a potential client that morning. She hummed cheerfully as she guided the vacuum around the glass coffee table.

With deft movements, she tilted the vacuum upright so it locked in place. She continued to hum despite the perpetual whirring of the machine. She ran the sleeve of her t-shirt across her face, then bent to lift the black square cushions off the couch.

Joni stared down at the couch, feeling her jaw creep open with surprise. In between the couch cushions had been remnants of a granola bar, a dollar in change, and yet another black-handled steak knife from the kitchen.

She slowly reached behind her and flipped the switch of the vacuum. The machine grew silent. Joni tilted her head, staring down at the knife, puzzled. Was it Tate who was messing with her? Or Adrian?

"Boys," she sighed, and once more took the knife into the kitchen.

But it hadn't ended there.

Joni began to find the black-handled streak knives all over the house. One in the medicine cabinet in the bathroom, one amongst the pens Tate kept on his desk, one on top of the door to the basement. Any semblance of humor the joke once had quickly evolved into perversion.

"Just tell me who is doing it. I promise I won't get mad," Joni said as she bit into her pizza crust.

She had found a steak knife every day over the last two weeks. Avery had already finished her dinner and gone back upstairs to play with her dolls, but Tate and Adrian still sat at the table. A white, grease-laden plate sat in front of each of them.

Adrian took her seriously, whereas Tate merely laughed at her.

"Steak knives? Who has the time to do that?" he lifted his hand, palm upward, at the thought. He turned to his son with a suspicious glance.

"Don't look at me, I didn't do it," Adrian said with a flick of his shoulders.

Joni tossed the remaining portion of her crust onto the plate in front of her with a thud. "Well, one of you guys must be lying, and I'm telling you that it isn't funny anymore," she scowled.

The following morning, Joni was on the phone with her potential client when she stepped on one of Avery's dolls. Pain shot up her leg as she cussed quietly to herself. The two-inch doll stared up at her from the floor, looking pitiful.

After she hung up, she grabbed an empty shoebox from the coat closet and marched about the house. There was evidence of Avery everywhere, from a discarded rainbow colored sock by the television to a fake Barbie phone in the kitchen. One by one the items went into the shoebox, which Joni carried up the stairs to Avery's room.

The pink gauze curtains were still closed, casting the room in a filmy, rose colored hue. She navigated around clothes and toys on the bubblegum colored carpet until she got to her daughter's white daybed, tucked in the farthest corner from the door.

Joni set the box down and turned to leave the room when something glinted in her peripheral vision. She stopped mid-stride and looked around. Avery had a small bookcase which was primarily filled with Junie B. Jones books, a miniature set of chairs around an equally small, round oak table, and the dollhouse that Tate had made for her on her fifth birthday.

Joni readjusted her position until she caught the reflective surface again, beaming up at her from within the dollhouse. She walked over and crouched in front of the three-story home. She remembered how many late nights Tate had put into building it. He had been so meticulous, and it showed in every miniaturized roof tile. Her eyes moved from room to room until she saw it—a steak knife.

With a shaky hand, she picked it up from the second level of the dollhouse and began to cry. Finding a knife in the laundry had been odd. Finding them around the house had been unnerving. But finding them in her daughter's room was downright horrifying.

Joni stared at the knife in her hand as it grew blurry and distorted. The joke had been taken one step too far.

Suddenly, she stopped crying. Tate and Adrian loved Avery, and were very protective of her. Leaving a knife in her dollhouse was just too uncharacteristic of them to be ignored.

She hadn't considered Avery as the culprit because so many of the knives had been up high. But her daughter knew where the stepstool was. It was not out of the question.

Joni groaned and slowly made her way down the stairs, wondering how she and Tate could possibly handle the bizarre situation.

When he got home, the two agreed to tag team Avery that night at dinner. Tate made lasagna in the oven while Joni brought a stack of plates to the table. Adrian set cutlery by each one. Avery sat in her designated chair, swinging her legs to and fro under the table as she starred at her pink, sparkly cup. Cinderella was printed on it, but she had grown pale with age.

Wearing two floral oven mitts, Tate picked up the glass casserole dish and carefully placed it in the center of the table. He used a black plastic spatula to cut each of them a healthy portion which he dropped onto their plates.

"Looks good, Dad," Adrian said as he sat opposite his sister.

Avery looked at the many layers of her lasagna as if she were dissecting it. Joni brought a forkful to her mouth before she made eye contact with her husband. A question gleamed in his dark eyes.

Joni took another bite of her meal and slowly chewed as she considered how to begin. Tate was always the gentler of the two, but Joni was better at articulating what needed to be said. Many of the serious talks they had had with their children in the past had been led by her.

"Avery, sweetie," she said—she could already hear a nauseating sweetness to her tone. "I was putting some toys back in your room today when something caught my eye by your dollhouse."

Avery looked at her mother, her brown eyes not registering alarm. Joni faltered and looked to Tate, who nodded at her encouragingly.

"Well, I found a knife in your dollhouse. Now, I promise I won't get mad, but you have to tell me why you keep leaving knives all over the house," Joni said, looking at her daughter sternly.

Avery tapped her fork against her plate. A small wrinkle appeared right above the bridge of her nose. "What knife?" she asked.

"Like this one," Tate supplied, showing Avery the skinny dinner knife he had in his right fist. "The ones you know you aren't supposed to touch until you're a couple years older," he added, giving his daughter a knowing expression.

Avery tossed her fork with a clatter. She looked at both of her parents as if they had just grounded her for a year. "But I don't touch those knives!" she wailed. "I only use the plastic ones Mom got from IKEA. I don't have any knives in my room!"

Adrian quietly cut into a section of his lasagna, watching his sister's body language. She stared directly into their parents' eyes. Her shoulders were spread out, open, and she didn't nervously tap with her fingers or her toes either.

"Honey, are you doing this because you're lonely? Because if so, I understand—" Tate began, before Avery shrieked over him.

"I swear I didn't do anything! I don't even know where Mommy keeps those knives," she said. Her round cheeks grew flushed, and tears began to collect at the bottom of her lashes.

"Then how do you explain how a knife not only got into your dollhouse, but in the laundry and on top of the basement door?" Joni retorted, flinging her arms wide in frustration.

Immediately, Avery stopped crying. She looked at her mother with wide eyes and her nostrils flared out when she exhaled. "The basement door?" she whispered.

"Yeah, it was right on top of the door as it stood open a few days ago," Adrian replied.

Avery looked to her brother. He saw her hands, pale and small, begin to quiver on the tabletop. "The basement," she whispered to herself, looking helplessly down at her plate.

"Honey, I understand that you want to be able to play games like your dad and your older brother, but I need you to stay away from the knives and from that horrible basement, okay? Especially when you use the step ladder," Joni said, trying to be kind and casual. She hated being permanently stuck with the role of disciplinarian.

"Mom, I didn't go near the basement, I swear," Avery pleaded. "It must have been the thing from under the stairs."

Had a pin dropped in the Harrison kitchen at that moment, every family member would have heard it crash to the floor. Joni stared at her daughter, Tate stared at his wife, and Adrian took turns staring at both parents, wondering what in the world they would say. Everybody's lasagna was growing cool on their plates.

"Av, I know it's easy to lay blame on your imaginary friend, but the easy way isn't always the right way," Joni finally said, her eyebrows disappearing into her loose bangs.

Avery rammed the heel of her right shoe into one of the table's legs. "He isn't imaginary and he isn't my friend! He's mean!" she bellowed at her mom.

"Avery Rose, you lower your tone right now," Tate said, looking pointedly at her. He so rarely made demands from his kids that she complied instantly.

With a fleeting look of frustration, Joni rose from her chair and began to pace alongside the stove. Her daughter had been many things thus far in her life. She had been loud, emotional, dramatic and self-centered... but she had never lied to any serious degree. Joni had no idea how to handle the situation, and so she decided to pace. At least, until she came up with something.

"Av, have you been making new friends at school?" Adrian asked. He used his fork to peel back layers of his lasagna and separate them onto his plate.

"Yeah. Why?" Avery asked. She stared at her brother's plate, momentarily mesmerized by what he was doing.

"Those girls from Mrs. Baine's class, Molly and Erin, are still around?"

"Yeah. Why?" Avery asked again, this time with some urgency.

Adrian shrugged and slowly began to put his lasagna back together again. "I don't know, I've just read that when a child develops an imaginary friend it's because they're lonely."

Avery glared up at her brother. He could see her gritting her teeth together as her temper surged. "It... is not... imaginary!" she howled, then pushed against the table with her palms so her chair would scoot backward. She jumped from the chair and stomped her way through the kitchen.

"It is not imaginary. It is real, and it is awful!" she said, then disappeared through the doorway towards the stairs.

Joni stared at the stainless steel oven, looking as though she might cry as well. "That did not go over well," she whispered.

Tate made a grunting noise as he wedged his fork into his lasagna. "Don't worry about it, Jo. She will be fine in no time. She always is."

Joni shook her head and suppressed a sob. She got up and walked to the corner cabinet, where she kept a couple of bottles of wine. She pried the cork out with a corkscrew and reached into one of the gray cupboards for a glass.

"Chances are, now that you've confronted her, she will probably confess in a couple hours anyway," Adrian said, reaching for the salad bowl. "That outburst was due to guilt, not anger."

Joni poured some of the Moscato into the glass and returned to the kitchen table. "I hope you're right, Ad," she said, running a hand through her tousled hair. "When Avery is mad the whole world is punished."

Tate chewed a mouthful of lasagna as he stared at the white damask wallpaper, lost in thought. "Hmm," he murmured as he chewed.

Joni and Adrian turned to face Tate. A small glob of marinara sauce was caught in his beard. His gaze roamed to his wife, and he blinked in surprise as he found her staring at him expectantly.

"What?" he asked with a shrug of his shoulders.

"It sounded like you had something to say," Joni replied with an amused grin on her face.

Tate ran his tongue along his teeth as he placed his fork and knife onto the table and leaned back in his wooden chair. "I'm just interested in hearing more about this supposed creature under the stairs, that's all," he said. His tone was meek with uncertainty.

"To what end?" Joni asked with a quick shake of her head. Her earrings, which were gold and dangly, swung from side to side.

"Well, what if she's telling the truth? Or thinks she is, anyway," Tate said. His mouth became an inquisitive line across his face. "What if she really thinks she is seeing something under the stairwell?"

Joni blinked and stared down at the table, contemplating this alternative theory. Her shoulders seemed to grow heavier with every passing moment. "If that is the case, then it means that Avery is suffering from hallucinations, and we have a bigger problem than we all thought," she said quietly.

Adrian looked down at his half-eaten meal, picturing his sister in his mind. The two of them had never been very much alike. Where Adrian was quiet and curious, Avery liked to be smack in the middle of the spotlight, in the mix of everything around her. She had a penchant for theatrics, and showmanship, and as her older brother, Adrian often found her to be both mentally and physically taxing.

Nevertheless, they had a good relationship, despite their abundant differences and their abundant age gap. Buried deep within Avery's desire to be the center of the universe was a good person. Adrian had seen glimpses of it, perhaps more than anyone. It appeared when someone was being picked on at the playground, or when someone attempted to cheat at a board game. Avery was crazy, but she was also fair.

She also tended to the tell the truth, not because it was expected of her, but due to her own moral compass.

"I hate to say it, but I don't think Avery is intentionally lying," Adrian said. "Which means that she is either suffering from some sort of disorder, or our house has a Casper."

Joni nodded and brushed a tear from her cheek. Tate sat up straighter in his chair and excitedly drummed his fingers on the armrests.

"Now, there's a thought," he murmured

Joni frowned at her husband. Her black eyeliner was smeared underneath her eyelashes. "What?" she asked. Her tone was flat and disheartening.

"What if our house is haunted?" Tate asked.

Adrian blinked slowly, while Joni made a snort of derision. "Please," she said. She looked almost amused.

Tate shrugged, but still retained a strange glimmer in his eye. "Think about it. People deal with haunted houses all the time. It's a pretty common occurrence."

"Yeah, in television shows!" Joni retorted, staring at her husband in disbelief.

"Sure, there are fabrications and exaggerations," he said, dipping his head. "But they're on television because it happens to people in real life, all the time.

Adrian cleared his throat. "Dad, you know I have more of an interest in the paranormal than a lot of people, so I don't want you to feel like I'm not open to the idea," he said politely. "But the fact of the matter is that Avery is the only one who has experienced anything out of the ordinary. Doesn't that sort of leave you with the impression that something is wrong with Avery and not the house?"

Tate bit his lip. He chewed for a few moments before he slapped his palm against the table, causing his wife to flinch in her seat.

"Aha!" he cried, then looked at Joni apologetically. "Sorry, Jo. But there *has* been one other person who is experiencing something unusual in this house."

"Who?" Joni inquired.

"You," Tate replied, becoming quite animated. "That strange noise in the hall that we have no logical explanation for." He beamed at his wife as though he had just purchased her a new car.

Joni snorted again, her face completely devoid of tears. "You yourself said that this is an extremely old house. All that is, is the house settling." She took a large sip of her wine and tried her best to ignore the fact that not long before she had been finding holes in the very theory she now defended. What Tate proposed was preposterous.

Adrian sighed and plunged his fork into the lettuce that covered one half of his plate. It wasn't often that his parents fought, but when they did they did not feel compelled to hide it from their oldest offspring. While this made Adrian feel like an adult, it also made him feel like the proverbial fly on the wall.

"Maybe we should just talk to her... get her to tell us about this supposed 'thing,'" he suggested mildly. "Maybe the way she talks about it or describes it will help us determine how best to handle it."

Joni nodded appreciatively. "I think that's a great idea," she said, and finished the last of her wine.

"I do too," Tate said. "So much so that I'm going to ask her about it myself," he nodded briskly.

"You don't think we should do it as a family?" Joni frowned.

Adrian interjected. "Actually, it should be Dad. He's the only one Avery ever lets into her room when she's upset. He can get her to talk."

Joni sighed but nodded in assent. "Worth a shot," she said.

CHAPTER NINE

Tate rapped his knuckles against the door to Avery's room the following morning. She had only come out to use the bathroom and to sneak snacks up from the kitchen.

"Who is it?" Avery asked. Tate could hear her scowl through the words.

"Just Dad," Tate replied, forcing his voice to sound chipper.

Avery hesitated for a moment, then finally told him he could come in.

At 6'2", Tate was fairly used to being the tallest guy in the room, but Avery's room always made him feel like he was Hagrid or something. Everything felt minuscule as he tiptoed between trinkets strewn across the floor and over to the edge of her bed.

Avery remained in the corner, holding up a doll in each hand side by side, as if they were walking together.

"Not making your brother play Ken's part?" Tate smiled.

"Not today," Avery replied tersely.

Tate fidgeted with a purple flower sewn onto Avery's comforter. A piece of plum colored thread got caught in his hangnail and he yanked his hand across his body. One of the embroidered filigrees on the blanket lost a couple of inches of string. Tate shook the mess off his hands and hoped his daughter wouldn't notice.

"Listen, Av, your mom and I… we don't think you're lying," he said softly.

Avery continued to make her Barbie dolls hop forward, but he had caught her attention.

"If you say it's this thing, well, okay, it is. But we are going to need your help. You're the only one who knows what it looks like."

Avery stared up at her father and looked as though she was about to speak when something caught her attention in the doorway. She opened her palms and let her dolls fall unceremoniously to the floor. Tate watched his daughter grow pale as she stared, wide-eyed, into the hallway.

"Av? You okay?" Tate asked. He sunk down to the floor and crawled over Avery's bright pink carpet to crouch beside her. The moment he sat down, Avery blinked her eyes and turned to look back at him. The abundant horror had left her eyes, but he read a lingering sense of fear in her other features.

"What did you see?" Tate asked. He leaned in and wrapped his arms around her tiny shoulders.

A wave of cold flowed up Avery's spine and she suppressed a shudder. "It was the thing. It was walking in the hallway," she whispered. "You'll have to talk quietly, or else it will hear you."

Tate nodded and placed his index finger against his lips. "What does it look like?" he asked.

Avery hesitated, glancing back up at the doorway. "It changes when it wants to. Most of the time I don't see it. It likes to speak to me from the bottom of the stairs, where it gets dark."

Tate frowned down at the pink carpet by his feet. "If it speaks to you from the bottom of the stairs, how can it pinch your ankles when you walk down them?" he reasoned.

Avery was nonplussed. "He doesn't need to be in his body to hurt people," she whispered.

Tate grimaced. It hurt to hear his daughter speak in such a way. He scratched the back of his neck, feeling less sure of himself than he had since he first started dating Joni. "Why is it doing this?" he asked. He wasn't sure if he addressed the question to Avery or himself.

Avery shook her head. Her brown hair, thick and wavy like her mother's, hung on either side of her face. "I don't know," she whispered back. "I made it really mad."

Her voice quivered. Tate gripped her shoulders more tightly. "This is not your fault, baby," he said fiercely, as Avery choked back a small sob. "Av, I need you to tell me exactly what the thing said about the basement."

She gulped in air, but nodded. "It had been pinching me for a couple days," she began in hushed tones. "I would look behind me at each step, but I never saw anything. Then one day, as I walked down the stairs it told me to come into the kitchen."

Avery's voice broke again, but she ignored the tear that spilled from the corner of her left eye. "I was scared, but I couldn't help it. I had to go to the kitchen. When I got there, I heard something breathing from behind the basement door. I tiptoed to the door and looked down the stairs, but it was too dark to see anything. And that's how I knew it was there," she whispered.

"What did it say to you, Avery?" Tate asked, both wanting to hear the answer and fearing it.

"It said I should come down the stairs to play," Avery replied. She dipped her head down towards her chest, feeling ashamed.

"And you said no, right?"

Avery nodded slowly. "I don't like the basement. It's dark and scary down there."

"And what did… the thing… say to you after that?" Tate asked.

Avery bit her lip in much the same way he himself did. "It said that if I didn't I would be sorry."

Tate frowned down at the carpet, feeling dread creep through his body as if he were sinking into ice water. Had Avery developed the imaginary being to get attention, she probably would have been more forthcoming about it, or how it interacted with her. But getting her to discuss the thing was like pulling teeth.

Which left a haunting. Or a hallucination.

"Did it say what it would do if you didn't play with it?" Tate asked softly.

Avery shook her head, looking solemn. "All I know is that I don't want to know," she said, and her face crinkled as she began to cry in earnest.

Tate pulled her head to his chest and ran his hands through her hair. He could feel a combination of her tears and snot sink through his button-down shirt and onto his skin. The joys of parenthood.

"I'm sorry," Avery blubbered. She clutched onto him with short fingers and tiny nails.

"It's okay. I got you. I believe you," Tate told his daughter. And then he realized what he said was true.

***

"No way. There's no way," Joni said, tossing her hands up into the air. She stood in the doorway between her and Tate's bedroom and their private bath. She stared up at her husband, rubbing lotion into her hands. He was on the other side of the bed, reaching into their dresser for pajamas.

He shrugged and shut the drawer as he tossed a pair of flannel pants onto the bed. "I'm not saying it's likely. I just don't want to entirely rule it out," he reasoned.

His wife walked over and sank onto her side of the bed. She leaned back into her goose-down pillows as she watched her husband change into his pajamas. "You're saying you find it more likely that our house is haunted than that a seven-year-old girl is unhappy that we moved and is now suffering from some kind of delusion due to the stress?" she asked incredulously.

Tate ran his hand through his hair with a nervous chuckle. "Well, when you put it that way…" He lunged forward on the bed until he was sprawled on his stomach. He reached out and took one of Joni's hands in his.

He looked at her, all trace of humor gone from his face. "If you're asking me whether or not I know how to proceed, I can readily tell you that I don't know," he said quietly. "But no matter what, I don't want our daughter thinking that she is crazy, or that her parents don't believe in her."

Joni opened her mouth, then closed it again. Finally, she just gave him a nod and a compassionate smile. It was hard to argue with his reasoning—he operated from such a kind perspective. It was one of the reasons she had fallen in love with him in the first place.

Tate smiled and ran his fingers slowly along her jawline. "Just keep an open mind, okay?" he asked in a whisper.

"Okay," she whispered back.

CHAPTER TEN

From that night forward, the Harrisons all attempted to keep an open mind as to the thing that lived under the stairs. They didn't encourage Avery to mention it, but they never censored her either.

She avoided the corner of the kitchen that was closest to the basement stairs at all costs. She also often asked one of her family members to bring things—a bottle of water, a hairbrush—up to her room after dark. "I don't want to hear the thing whispering as I go down," Avery whimpered.

Adrian had multiple conversations with his younger sister about the matter. He once sat at her junior sized table and chairs for an hour, sipping imaginary tea with Avery's stuffed bear so he could ask her questions.

"It's telling me not to talk to you," Avery said bluntly. She adjusted the straw colored sunhat that sat on her head. "He doesn't like you very much," she added. Her tone was sheepish and apologetic.

"So it's a he?" Adrian asked, his straight black eyebrows quirked in interest.

Avery sipped imaginary tea from her plastic tea cup as she contemplated the question. "I guess," she hesitated. "I don't know. Its body is all black and shadowy."

She glanced nervously towards the hall, then leaned over the table towards her brother. "I don't think we should talk about it anymore," she added.

Adrian nodded. He continued to watch his sister pretend to fill their cups.

That night he lay down in his bed and reviewed his notes. As he re-read his observations of his sister, he amused himself by contemplating a career in psychology.

She was consistent in her descriptions of the physical characteristics of the thing. She did not exhibit any other notable signs of mental instability: no sudden changes in mood or personality. Nothing quite made sense.

Adrian sighed and set his notebook down on his lap. Perhaps he was not educated enough to recognize any potential signs. Or perhaps Avery had developed into a very talented liar after all.

Theories and questions floated in his mind until his eyelids grew heavy and the room around him grew hazy.

Several hours later, Adrian felt sunlight on his face, slowly warming up his room. His eyelashes fluttered as he gained consciousness and stared up at the glossy white ceiling of his bedroom.

As he stretched, flashes of images from his last dream flooded his brain. He had dreamt of a simple door, made out of cherry mahogany. Its white trim and modern silver handle were a dead giveaway: it was the door to their basement.

His eyes had fixated on it for what felt like hours. Time seemed to speed up, as the light shifted from one side to the other. First it was washed in tones of orange and yellow, but they quickly deepened into hues of blue and purple as the sun set. That was all. Just blank white walls, a dark wooden floor and their basement door—which was closed and yet felt very much open.

Adrian shook his head and furiously rubbed at his eyes. Scattered all over the floor of his room were dozens of sheets of notebook paper. They were spread out on the light beige carpet without any discernible pattern. It looked as though they had blown that way.

Realizing they were from the notebook he had bought just five days prior, Adrian looked at his desk. He swore he had placed the notebook beside his keyboard. Everything appeared normal, apart from its absence.

His blinds made a clacking sound as they struck against the window sill. He couldn't sleep in silence. He habitually left the window open a few inches while he slept, bringing the noise of the night into his bedroom. A strong wind had spread through Ely, and lake houses felt it especially. Adrian looked from the open window to his desk and grimaced.

He tossed the covers aside and stepped onto the carpet. His toes touched the torn edge of one of the strewn papers. He crouched down and reached for it. The flimsy piece flipped over as it fell back to the carpet.

Adrian flinched as he saw that the sheet of paper had writing on it. In large, looping, childlike letters was the word 'geduld.'

Adrian had seen his fair share of Expressionist films, and he believed the word to be German in origin.

"But who wrote it?" he asked himself.

With a deep sense of foreboding, Adrian grabbed another sheet of paper and turned it around. Same word, same childish handwriting.

Frantically, Adrian grabbed for each of the papers near him. They all had the word 'geduld' written in the center. He stared up from the last sheet and looked around his room. There were so many pages he could hardly see his carpet. Staring at them made all the little hairs on the back of his neck begin to rise.

He immediately stood up and walked over the paper into the hallway. He leaned against the light blue wall beside the doorframe until his legs slowly gave out and he sank to the floor. Adrian put his head in his hands and took several deep breaths.

He was being silly. He was making correlations between the prank and his creepy dream. Adrian chuckled softly to himself. Obviously his dream about the door was because of his conversation with Avery about the thing. And clearly Avery had written on the papers and spread them all over his room. It was likely her way of getting back at him for not defending her in front of their parents.

Adrian stroked his chin absentmindedly. Why had his sister chosen a German word, though?

"Because she wants me to think it was the thing," he murmured out loud. Slowly, he got to his feet and turned back into his bedroom. He spent the next seven minutes bending down to grab each sheet of paper and stacking them neatly in a pile. He had already decided that he wouldn't tell his parents about the incident. If Avery was doing this for attention, then telling them about it would only please her more.

It was best to confront her alone.

Adrian walked out of his room and turned left down the long, narrow hallway. He passed the double doors that led to his parents' room on the right, and the green and white bathroom he shared with his sister on the left. His sister's room was on the opposite side of the house. He padded across the carpet and put his ear to her door.

It sounded completely quiet.

Adrian reached for the long silver handle and inched it downward. He slowly pushed the door open. A small amount of light from the hall shone onto Avery's baby pink carpet. At the center of the farthest wall was Avery's bed—a twin sized white four-poster bed with a gauzy canopy.

Through the film, Adrian saw his younger sister asleep on her side, under a rainbow colored blanket. He crept up and sat beside her. Locks of brown hair were spread across her pillow as she breathed with her mouth open.

He put his hand on her shoulder and gently began to shake her back and forth.

"Avery. Hey, Avery! Wake up," he hissed.

Avery tossed and murmured incoherently. She was asleep again within seconds.

Adrian nudged her shoulder until Avery slowly opened her eyes and squinted up at him.

"Adrian? What are you doing in here? What time is it?" she asked, yawning. He could just barely see her scowling in the dark.

"It's almost seven, so Mom is going to be coming to wake you up in a few minutes anyway," Adrian whispered.

With a groan, Avery attempted to grab her comforter and pull it over her head. Adrian peeled it back down in an instant. "Seriously, I need to talk to you," he insisted. "I want to know why you're pulling pranks on me. You know I'm on your side."

Avery's mouth became a small round 'o' as she stared up at her brother, bewildered.

"What are you talking about? What prank?" she whined, and sat up. Her hair was coming out of a loose ponytail on the side of her head.

"In my room," Adrian snapped. "The papers all over my floor."

"*What*?" Avery asked. She gave him a look that was both confused and unnerved.

"Don't play dumb with me. You know what I mean. The papers," Adrian said. His shoulders slouched as she continued to stare at him as though he had grown another head. Adrian wasn't a particularly confrontational person, and he was even less so when it came to his sister—as annoying as she could, sometimes, be. Looking back into her brown eyes, he knew this was an argument he wasn't ever going to win.

"Forget it," he sighed, and stood up. He made his way to her door.

"I don't go in your room, you know!" Avery called feebly after him, to which he waved an impatient hand in her direction.

Later that day, Adrian found himself wondering about the incident as he passionlessly ate the uninspired cafeteria food at school. The room was a large white square, with industrial piping on the ceiling. An array of long, rectangular tables and their attached benches were laid out in a makeshift pattern on the white and blue tiled floor.

On his first day he had found one section of a table by a window to be empty, and claimed it for his own. It had been his spot ever since. He glanced out the window past the dense green lawn to the waiting area where the buses came to scoop up underclassmen every day when the final bell rang.

He pictured the sloppy cursive handwriting on the paper as he brooded over his meatloaf surprise. Avery was only seven, but she had really good penmanship. She had always admired Adrian's school essays and insisted on being taught how to write in cursive. Joni had bought her a practice pad which she and Adrian took turns critiquing. It had paid off.

There was no way the message could have been from Avery unless she was smart enough to purposefully make her handwriting different, over and over again no less. Adrian loved his younger sister, but she wasn't always the brightest crayon in the box. As she wrote on those dozens of dozens of pages, she would have been distracted by something… she would have started writing in her natural style.

He shook his shaggy black hair out of his eyes and peered around the cafeteria. A line of students looped around the opposite side of the room. In between them and Adrian was a herd of teenagers, some seated and eating, others walking from table to table socializing. It seemed so cliché, and yet Adrian could look around and identify several stereotypical social groups.

For one, you had your male varsity athletes, their hulking shoulders squished together underneath their various soccer, hockey and football uniforms, all in shades of blue and white.

At the adjacent table was where the popular kids perched, fixated on their gold iPhones and Coach purses. Adrian couldn't help but grin to himself. It didn't matter that he was seated in a school in the middle of nowhere northeast Minnesota. Teens were like this everywhere.

Adrian's gaze trailed to the small group of girls sitting at the other end of his table, closer to everyone else. One at the very end had long dark brown hair and was reading a German textbook. He looked at her until she felt it and looked back at him. He smiled tentatively. She had wide, bright blue eyes.

"Um, could I borrow your book by any chance?" he asked her.

The girl looked from him to her textbook. "Sure," she said. She placed the book on the table and slid it his way with a smile.

"Thank you," Adrian said. He pushed his bright orange cafeteria tray across the table, dragged the book to him and eagerly opened it up.

"Geduld, geduld, geduld," he chanted quietly to himself as he searched for a glossary. He turned the pages until he came across a list of terms. But geduld wasn't listed.

Adrian blinked down at the book for a moment before he began going through the pages again. The next segment after the glossary was an index. Using his index finger, Adrian trailed down the list until he got to 'ge.' There it was: geduld – pgs 147–148.

He skimmed through the book until he got to page 147. In the top right corner was what appeared to be a German toddler, crying and pointing to a neatly wrapped present.

Adrian's eyes roamed the page until he found the word in bold, black text. A puzzled frown returned to his face as he looked at the word and its English translation.

It meant patience.

CHAPTER ELEVEN

By the time Adrian took the steep steps up the school bus, he had changed his mind about the papers at least ten times. On one hand it wasn't likely his sister actually knew any German. Sure, she could have used the family computer, tucked into a corner of the family room, but Adrian was fairly certain she didn't even know how to spell patience.

And yet… if she hadn't done it, who had? Where was the logical explanation? By the time the bus screeched to a halt on Pioneer Road, Adrian knew what he had to do. The bi-fold bus doors groaned as the driver cranked them open.

"Thanks," Adrian murmured as he leapt off the bus. He hurried up the winding stone walk to the front porch and fiddled for his key in the pocket of his jeans. Once he was inside, he took the stairs two at a time up to his room. Sitting at his desk, he shook the black mouse to wake his computer.

Thus began an extensive yet relatively aimless search. A trail of Google searches in his wake, Adrian finally stumbled upon something that caught his attention: automatic writing. Where had he heard the term before? What did it even mean? He typed the words into the search bar and tapped the enter key with his index finger. Within seconds, a definition was sprawled across the top of the screen.

Automatic writing is an alleged supernatural ability to allow a spirit to temporarily possess the used of ones writing hand. Typically scribbles only appear, however proficient practitioners manifest beautiful writing often in script unlike their own.

The hair on the back of his neck stood on end as he read the definition over a second time. Whether it was his subconscious or something outside of him, he found the idea to be incredibly creepy.

Adrian shuddered and wiggled slightly in his desk chair. He mentally steeled himself and continued to read. His eyes roamed to one particular headline.

Automatic Writing: Spiritual Ability or the Sign of a Poltergeist?

Think you have been gifted with the strange ability to write while you are asleep? Well, think again! Many people who believe they are able to channel their subconscious while sleeping are actually the victim of a poltergeist that has invaded their home!

"Poltergeist?" Adrian murmured. Apart from the 80s horror movie, he wasn't really familiar with the term. Not in any in-depth way, at least.

With carefully placed fingers, Adrian typed the word into the search bar. Over the course of an hour he immersed himself in legend, explanations and infamous cases. He found it darkly ironic that the very term was German in origin. A 'noisy ghost.' He thought about his mother's insistence that something kept making noise in the hallway.

Adrian took a deep breath and turned his monitor off with a sense of finality. He was clearly losing his grip, convincing himself that their house was haunted. He looked at his two large, cheerful windows and the luxurious folds of the plaid comforter spread across his bed with a laugh. Since his mother's massive redecorating efforts, their house was about as creepy as curdled milk. He was being absurd.

Shaking his head, he got up to find where he had placed his backpack. It was time to do something logical, like homework. It was time to come back to reality.

And yet Adrian found that, come a few hours later, he couldn't sleep. He anxiously imagined a litany of horrible things. He lay in bed, listening for the sounds of scratching in the hallway. The sound of unseen footsteps making the floorboards creak in his bedroom. A phantom voice, whispering harsh things in his ear.

Logically he knew that poltergeists didn't exist, and yet... He turned over upon his bed, wrestling with the blankets. He stared up at the ceiling in hesitation for a moment before he scrambled out of bed and crept into the dimly lit hall.

He stared down the curving staircase where the light didn't reach. The staircase itself was very beautiful, with an ornate railing. Joni had painted it white, but its shape and style were undeniably antique.

Adrian stared down into the darkness and took a tentative step down. Then another step. And another. Each tread had its own unique creaking pattern under his weight. Where did Avery say it pinched her? He took a deep breath and took two more steps. Goose bumps formed along his forearms, and he chastised himself for his fear. It was an ordinary staircase in an ordinary house, occupied by a troubled young girl. Nothing more.

He let out a brief chuckle and bounded down two more steps—and then he felt something thin and sharp dig into his right ankle. The pain seized him at once, and he gave a yelp of pain and surprise. Adrian half tumbled down the remaining seven steps and came to an abrupt halt at the bottom. He clutched at his heart over his black and red Deftones t-shirt as he looked back up the stairs.

"Holy shit," he whispered in the dark.

It took the seventeen-year-old a good ten minutes to work up the courage to use the stairs again. He used his hands to propel himself upward, his feet thumping on each step as he ran. He didn't stop running until he was back inside his bedroom, watching all corners of the room from the relative safety of his bed.

His brain insisted over and over again that it just wasn't possible, that there was some other explanation. But the nauseous churning of his stomach and the racing of his heart told him a different story entirely.

CHAPTER TWELVE

The following morning Adrian found Avery standing in her bedroom, gently brushing her thick brown hair in the oval mirror above her dresser. He cleared his throat as he stood on the edge of her pink carpet, attempting to appear humble.

"Alright if I come in?" he asked.

Avery stared coldly at his reflection in the mirror. "Fine," she sniffed. She looked haughty as she resumed running the bristled brush through her hair.

Adrian walked to her bed and sat down so he faced her. He picked up one of her decorative pillows and stared down at it. He idly began to knead its magenta fabric.

"I felt the pinch last night."

Adrian jerked his head up as Avery's wooden hairbrush clattered against the top of her dresser and thudded to the floor. She gaped at her brother in surprise, her anger gone.

"You did?" she whispered.

"I did," Adrian nodded with a sigh. "I spent all night trying to come up with some other explanation. Couldn't come up with a thing."

Avery looked at her brother, her expression melting into one of empathy. "It was scary, wasn't it?" she asked.

Adrian nodded slowly, picturing himself staring down the darkened staircase again. He realized that had he believed Avery before, he would never have been brave enough to try it. Suddenly, he understood all too well why Avery had always made their parents or him retrieve things from the first floor after dark.

Avery reached out and gently tapped him on the back of his hand, breaking him out of his chilling reverie. A green beaded bracelet she wore on her wrist slid against his fingers.

"What do we do?" she asked, looking solemn.

"Well…" Adrian said, scratching the back of his neck. "We need to start by really figuring out who—or what—this is. I know you've seen it. What can you tell me about it?"

Avery, who had bent to pick up her hairbrush, rose back up, frantically shaking her head. "Please don't make me talk about it," she pleaded. "I feel like it knows when I do."

"I'm sorry, but we must," he grimaced. "I can't figure out how to get rid of it if I don't know what it is, Av. I know it's scary, but telling me what you know about it could really help."

Avery slumped as she walked to the bed and sat beside her brother. She took a deep breath and then turned toward him. Her legs dangled several inches from the floor.

"It doesn't really have a face. Not one I can see, anyway," she began softly, suddenly seeming much too serious to be only seven. "I don't see it so much as I sense it around me. It follows me around the house."

Avery bore her eyes into her brother's. "It watches us when we eat at the kitchen table. Did you know that? It likes to peek at us from around the corner in the family room."

"How do you know it's actually peeking when you can't see it? Maybe it's just hovering in the other room?" Adrian pressed.

But Avery shook her head. "I can hear it thinking sometimes," she admitted. "I can hear its voice in my head. It's deep, like someone who is trying to talk to you from underwater."

"What does it say?" her brother asked.

"Not nice things," she said with a slow shrug of her left shoulder. "Since I told it I wouldn't play in the basement, it likes to say mean things, harsh things."

Adrian could hear her voice crack with emotion. He bit back the urge to stop questioning her. It was the only way. "What does it say to you, Av?" he whispered.

A tear brimmed from her right eye and slowly rolled down her cheek. "That it's going to hurt you and Mom and Dad. That things have just begun. That things will get worse."

Adrian put an arm around his sister as she ran one of her hands under her nose, sniffling. He found their unorthodox visitor completely frightening, and all he had endured was a small pinch to one of his feet. He could never imagine sensing the entity throughout the house.

He looked down at his sister. The skin under her eyes was a faint bluish purple, and her skin looked sallow. It was clear she wasn't sleeping well. How she could sleep at all was anybody's guess.

A lull of silence took over the room. Adrian looked around at his younger sister's decorative efforts. Practically every item in her room, from the ruffled curtains on the window to the pile of stuffed animals in the corner, was in sickening shades of pink and lilac. A small fragment of his brain found it darkly amusing that this was the room in which such a creepy subject was discussed.

"How many times have you seen—I mean… encountered—it?" he asked, as he tossed the pillow behind him, with the rest of them.

Avery squinted her eyes in thought. "I don't know," she said. "It's always there… here. I feel like I can always sense it in the house, even when it isn't near me. It likes the staircase, but it moves around a lot."

"Especially at night," she added in a different tone. It was one mixed with fear and weariness.

"What does it do at night, besides the pinching?"

Avery shrugged again, uncertainly. "It likes to go through our stuff."

"Go through our stuff?" he repeated.

"Yeah," she nodded. She began to fidget with her hair. "I hear it going through the cupboards in the kitchen, whispering to itself."

Adrian felt as if a dozen dead hands were on his back, running their fingers along his spine. Measure by measure, he was piecing information together, and the more he knew, the less he wanted to.

Was it a ghost? Was it some man who had lived and died in the house before Aunt Marie had acquired the property? Or was it, as Adrian both feared and predicted, no human spirit at all, but an otherworldly thing?

Adrian slowly stood up from the bed and walked in a tight circle in the center of Avery's room. Ghosts, while definitely unnerving, seemed simple in comparison. Every ghost hunting show that he had ever seen seemed to offer a variety of sure-fire tricks to expunge a dead soul from a house. Crosses, holy water, a cleaning ritual performed by a local priest. There was practically an index of ready solutions.

But if it was a poltergeist... From what he had gathered on the internet, some people believed that poltergeists were once living humans. And yet many others were convinced that these invisible spirits had never been human.

When Adrian added everything up, it was impossible to deny that the 'thing' was likely a poltergeist. It wasn't visible to the naked eye, unlike a ghost. They were most often identified by their penchant for moving objects around wherever they dwelt. He remembered how Joni kept finding steak knives in random nooks and crannies of the house.

Worst of all, while ghosts were usually passive in nature, poltergeists were known to prey on humans. Adrian and Avery had the marks on their ankles to prove it. He ceased his pacing and turned to look at his sister.

"How have you not been sitting in a corner with a blanket over your head?" he wondered.

Avery continued to play with her hair as she raised one shoulder up in a shrug. "I've seen *The Sixth Sense*, you know," she replied softly. "It was last year and you and Mom and Dad all thought I had gone to bed and put it on the TV. I remember crawling down the stairs and watching the whole thing as I lay on the carpet behind the sofa."

Adrian grinned a little at her confession. He remembered that day. It had been a muggy, rainy Sunday evening in Florida and one of the few occasions where everyone was at home at the same time. He remembered his mother spearing broccoli on her fork at dinner and suggesting that they all watch a movie together. It had been *The Incredibles* when Avery was awake, and *The Sixth Sense* after Tate had tucked her into bed.

"Av? That's nice and all, but what's your point?" he asked.

Avery looked down at her blanket and picked at a piece of thread. "I just remember that when Cole was being haunted by the dead, hiding in fear never seemed to help," she said.

With his sister's oddly wise words running through his mind, Adrian walked down the hall and stepped into his own room. He paused at the threshold and stared. There were sheets of notebook paper all over the floor again. They were lined up in rings, reminiscent of the rings you'd find within a tree.

His mouth agape, Adrian tentatively walked into his room and kneeled in front of the outermost ring. His hand was shaky as he reached out and took ahold of one of the corners of a sheet. He slowly turned it over.

Staring back at him were the same looping, child-like letters, but this time the words were in English.

Hello Adrian

CHAPTER THIRTEEN

Twenty minutes later, the Harrison family were all standing in Adrian's room, each at a loss for words. Avery leaned against the doorframe, her eyelids heavy as she stared grimly down at the rings of paper. Joni stood next to her son, with her arms crossed firmly across her chest. From the corner of his eye, Adrian could see her lips thinning out as she scowled. Tate was to the left of his wife, crouched on his sneakers, holding one of the pages in his hand.

Joni impatiently tapped her foot a couple of times on the beige carpet before she tossed both hands up in frustration. "Seriously guys, this is exhausting!" she snapped. "I'm sorry if this is some delayed act of revenge for moving, but you two cannot keep pulling these pranks on each other. I'm tired of it." She looked from one child to the next, looking to see if either of them showed an ounce of remorse or shame on their faces.

"It wasn't us, Mom," Adrian said. He looked at Joni with an expression he hoped would appear as open and sincere. She swallowed as her son continued to make unwavering eye contact. The urgency with which he tried to convince her was unsettling.

"And Adrian felt it on the staircase. It pinched him. I wasn't lying," Avery piped in from the doorway. Joni let out a huge sigh as she raised a hand to rub her forehead. She looked fed up, whereas Tate looked contemplative. His brow furrowed as he looked at the unfamiliar writing on the paper in his hand, and then up at his daughter. His brown eyes were assessing.

"You really felt it?" he asked Adrian.

"Yeah," Adrian murmured. His mouth sloped down in the corners as if in apology.

Joni sliced a hand through the air in front of her. "No, that is not what happened," she growled. "Avery has been stressed at school and because of the move, and she has started to imagine things as a result," she said, then turned to point at her son. "And you, who have been curious about these kinds of wacko things for a long time now, have succumbed to the power of suggestion. You began to think about it so much that you started to believe it was real yourself."

"No," Adrian retorted as his sister snapped, "That's not true!"

"Jo, you have to admit that this is all a little too bizarre to be quite normal," Tate said as he got back to his feet. His tone was honeyed and mild, almost as if he were speaking to someone on the ledge of a bridge.

Joni waved a hand dismissively at her husband. "Not normal doesn't necessarily equate to such extremes," she reasoned. "There is no scientific evidence that poltergeists are real!"

Adrian absentmindedly rubbed at his chin in thought. "But Stone Tape theory is becoming increasingly more valid in terms of proving that hauntings exist," he said, glancing at his mother. "If they can exist in the real world, why can't poltergeists?"

Joni ran her hands through her bangs as she groaned. "I can't talk to you people right now," she said. "I love you kids, but this whole prank, or hallucination, or whatever it is, has gone too far. It needs to stop, now."

She turned on her heels and marched out of the room. Adrian could hear her slippered footsteps walk down the hall to her bedroom. Tate sighed as he heard the door click shut.

"You guys promise this is not some prank?" he asked, looking sternly from Adrian to Avery.

"No, Daddy," Avery answered quietly. She looked to be on the verge of tears. Her bottom lip quivered as she toyed with the silver doorknob.

"This isn't my style," Adrian said. He shrugged at his dad as he shoved both hands into the pockets of his jeans.

"No," Tate nodded. He clapped a hand on his son's shoulder. "No, this definitely isn't—which is why I'm surprised your mother is so convinced that it is." He stared down at the rings again, the wrinkles reforming in between his eyebrows.

"We are in unchartered territory here," he added.

Adrian walked over to his black two-drawer nightstand and grabbed his smart phone. He touched the screen and enabled the camera. He held the phone up sideways and snapped several photos of the rings. Then he lowered himself down to the floor and flipped a page over so he could take a photo of the writing.

Tate watched, crossing his arms in front of his raspberry colored button-down shirt. "Collecting evidence?" he questioned.

Adrian shrugged and took another photo. "I suppose so, though who we would give it to I have no idea. Do priests handle poltergeists? I thought they only handled dead people and demons."

Tate chewed on his lower lip in thought. "Beats me," he admitted. "The only experience I have with these sorts of things is seeing *The Exorcist* and *Poltergeist* at the movie theater. I didn't even know that poltergeists *could* be non-human," he added with an irrepressible shudder.

Adrian jammed the phone into his pocket and began sliding the papers toward him into one pile, just as he had done the last time. "Do you know if Aunt Marie ever mentioned anything about the place being weird, or being scared, Dad?"

Tate walked over to Adrian's desk and perched on top of it, stretching his long legs out in front of him. "Not once," he replied, shaking his head. "And trust me, Aunt Marie was the type of person who would do so in a heartbeat. She was always going on these emotional tangents whenever I saw her. She was comical, but very dramatic."

"I'm scared," Avery admitted. She looked up at her father with pleading eyes, as if her confession alone could solve their problem.

"Come here, Av," Tate said as he opened his arms wide. Avery lunged forward and tossed herself into her father with all the power she could muster. He grunted with the added weight, but nevertheless wrapped his arms around her and kissed the top of her head.

"I got you, sweetie," he reassured her. "We are all in on this together, alright? We will figure this out together."

Adrian nodded and placed the stack of paper on his bedspread. "I think we can tackle this better if we split up duties, if you will. Dad, if you could try to convince Mom? We really need her to believe us."

"I agree," Tate said, stroking his daughter's hair in front of him.

"I will spend my lunch hours and my evenings conducting research. Maybe I can try to figure out how we can potentially get rid of it, or suppress it or something," Adrian said with uncertainty. He then glanced down at his sister, adopting a cautious demeanor.

"Avery…" he said, but trailed off. He scrunched up his face in discomfort.

"Yes…?" she replied, using the same uneasy tone. She looked up at her brother with an expression so distasteful he couldn't help but assume she knew what he would be asking.

"I know you're scared—I don't blame you. I'm actually incredibly impressed at how brave you're being," Adrian admitted with an attempt at a smile. "But I'm afraid you're going to have to endure the thing a little more. Any time you hear it speak in your head, or you encounter it somewhere in the house, I want you to write down what you experience. Maybe it will unwittingly divulge information that could help us."

Avery cringed at the thought, but nodded all the same. "If it will help get rid of it once and for all, then I'll do it."

Adrian clapped his hands together once. "We will figure this out, once and for all."

Joni was already asleep by the time Tate crept into their room and crawled into bed. He was asleep within a few minutes, but his evening ablutions had woken her up. She stared at the ceiling, listening to the methodical rumbles of her husband's snores. She could practically feel a wave of unhappiness begin at her toes and roll up her body.

Joni was the type of woman who prided herself on how tight-knit her family was. They had their moments of duress and strife like ordinary families, but nothing compared to the melodramatic tirades she heard from other mothers at school. Stephanie got pregnant, Tyler started experimenting with meth, Robbie was caught shoplifting… Joni tutted and consoled with the rest of them, but all the while she envisioned her two children donning golden halos as they finished their chores and completed their homework. She was blessed with having good children, who confided in her, who were not afraid to be seen in public with her.

But as Joni lay there in the dark, she couldn't muster up the imagery. Instead, she pictured both her children back in Adrian's room, staring up at her with mutinous expressions on their faces. Of course Tate had to side with them as well. She loved her husband's open spirit, his willingness to accept that all things were possible… but it always somehow made her into the bad guy. Joni was always the one who had to put her foot down, to insist on a reality check.

And now she was flying solo, the single voice of reason in an otherwise delusional family. How it had possibly come to this, she could not fathom.

Joni exhaled and slowly sat up in bed. She swung her legs over and stretched out her toes until she felt the edges of her slippers and dipped her feet into them. She shuffled out of the bedroom and down the long narrow hallway to the second floor landing.

Were pranks some new fad she hadn't heard about? She wondered as began to descend the steps. Generally, her family appreciated a good sense of humor. Each of them felt comfortable and inclined to joke and tease the others. But never to such an elaborate extent.

Or was it worse? Was it some stress-induced disorder each of her family members happened to be experiencing at the same time? They had all moved together, after all, and they were still very much adjusting to their new life. Was it some anxiety-ridden psychosis?

A sudden pain in her foot put a stop to her train of thought. She stared down at her feet, which glowed a pale white in the dark. The back of her left heel suddenly began to throb.

"You have got to be kidding me," she muttered out loud. She marched down the rest of the stairs shaking her head. That was the very phenomenon she had brought up to her family hours beforehand—the power of suggestion. Even the most stubborn of minds were susceptible. She could very well imagine that Avery had heard some chilling tale of a mythical ghost at school and that her fear, combined with heightened levels of stress, had culminated in some figment of her imagination. It was her fear in a bodied form. That was all.

Joni fumbled for the light switch at the bottom of the stairs. She glanced into the family room from the foyer. One of Avery's pink socks was on the tufted black leather sofa. Adrian had left his soccer ball under the glass coffee table.

"Kids," she sighed. She shuffled across the hardwood floor of the foyer and into the kitchen. Joni meandered around the island to the double doored fridge. She pulled the right door open and reached in, grabbing a carton of milk.

The cupboard to the left of the sink held their drinking glasses. She gingerly pulled one out and set it with a clink upon the counter. Ever since she had been little, whenever she found she couldn't sleep, she would sneak into the kitchen, get a glass of milk and sit at the table in the dark. Something about the ritual, perhaps the mere familiarity of it, was comforting.

Joni clutched her glass by the rim and carried it to the kitchen table. She sank into what was usually Avery's chair, though she wasn't sure why. As she slowly sipped at her milk, she amused herself by wondering how much it would cost to send an entire family to therapy each week. Would they receive a discounted group rate if they all went at the same time? Would she even need to go? Clearly, she was the only one who wasn't crazy…

She stared into the white liquid in her glass and felt sadder than she had in a very long time. Her life certainly hadn't been perfect, but if asked if, overall, it was more good than bad, Joni could answer in the affirmative without a moment's hesitation. Life had been good, even when it had been a struggle. Even when she'd realized she was pregnant with Avery and had to give up her schemes of owning her own interior design business. It had hurt—it had felt like a swift kick in the ass. But she'd had Tate to lean on, and Adrian had been so mature about the idea of not being the center of their world anymore. They got through it, they endured.

That time of their lives should have been much harder than what they were dealing with now. And yet, here she was feeling tears prick her eyes as she sat drinking milk by herself in the dark. An unexpected pregnancy and the sudden halt of her dream career had not made her falter then. But an elaborate story about an imaginary entity had her in shambles. It figured.

She was taking a swig from the glass when she heard something whack against the floor. It sounded as though something had fallen over in the family room. Joni grabbed her glass of milk and made her way back through the foyer.

She looked out into the family room and immediately dropped her milk. The cup plummeted to the wooden floor and smashed into pieces. Shards of glass spread out in a fan across the ground. Joni's hands went up to her face as she began to scream in shock.

Nothing seemed normal in the family room she had glanced at not five minutes before. The tufted black leather couch was where it usually was against the wall, but it was completely upside down. The two cloth armchairs Joni had bought to accompany the couch were also in their usual places, and also upside down.

Joni looked on in horror as one by one she realized that everything in the room was upside down, including a vase of lilies she had purchased the day before. The vase itself stood upside down on the upside-down coffee table. The flowers were in a broken, crumpled heap inside it.

The upside-down flat screen TV wobbled a little on the upside-down white credenza. The lamps, sleek silver pieces of three varying heights, all leaned against the walls, incapable of balancing on their rounded shades. Every plant, every trinket, every single DVD that had been in that room was meticulously overturned and tucked neatly back into place.

Joni began to feel her body tremble, from her pinky toes up to the nape of her neck. Faint whispering began to emanate from the darkened kitchen, causing her to jolt into the air in surprise. She clutched at the lapels of her terry cloth robe as she scanned the shadows.

She took a step back, then another. All she could see was a large square of darkness where the foyer opened up into the room, and yet… There was a creepy and incessant feeling as though there was something standing within that inky blackness, and as Joni tried to stare at it, it stared directly back.

CHAPTER FOURTEEN

Tate woke up to the sound of his wife screaming. Disoriented, he sat up in bed, attempting to discern what had interrupted his sleep. Another harsh scream from downstairs had him scrambling out of bed and running out of the bedroom.

He strode down the hallway and ran into something solid in the dark. He reached out by instinct and felt someone else's hand reaching towards him.

"Adrian?" Tate whispered.

"Yeah, it's me. Did I just hear—"

"Your mother? Yes. Let's go," Tate ordered, and made his way towards the stairs.

Adrian followed his father in silence. Neither of them had heard Avery's door click open as they spoke in the hallway. The scream had also woken her up, and she had peeked her head out to figure out what was wrong.

She listened to their exchange, then watched as their shadows moved towards the staircase. Avery had no intention of following, but as she stared out into the dark, empty hall, she realized she was all alone on the second floor. She thought about the thing and ran for the stairs.

As Tate, Adrian and Avery descended, they each felt the inevitable pinch on the seventh stair. Tate hesitated for a moment, staring down at his bare feet in amazement. He had readily accepted the possibility that they were dealing with something paranormal in origin, but feeling the poltergeist's phantom touch made it real. Goose bumps broke out all over his arms as he considered the ramifications, but he continued to rush down the stairs, thinking of his wife.

Joni had sunk down with her back against the front door, sobbing with her hands wrapped around her legs. She had subconsciously arranged her body to be as small as possible.

"Jo! Are you alright?" Tate asked, tossing himself to the ground in front of her. With an incoherent noise of relief, Joni wrapped her arms around her husband and cried into his shoulder in earnest.

Tate was too concerned about his wife to take in much of his surroundings. But Adrian and Avery stood in the foyer, looking into their family room with stunned disbelief on their faces.

"Dad," Adrian whispered.

Something about Adrian's tone caught Tate's attention as he craned his neck around to stare expectantly at his son. "What?" he barked.

He took in his son's pale complexion, his wide, startled eyes, and the way his finger trembled slightly as he pointed. "Look," he said.

Tate rose from the floor and looked at the chaos that was the family room. "Oh my God," he whispered. The magnitude of what the entity had done was overwhelming. He took a couple of steps back until he had his back against the wall, at a complete loss. It was small wonder his wife had screamed so much.

Joni hastened to her feet and walked to her husband. Seeing his reaction somehow pulled her out of her own mania. It was as if their bodies and minds had a secret pact that only one of them could be unhinged at any given time.

She gently placed a hand on Tate's forearm as he continued to stare, bewildered, at the scene before him. "What the hell happened?" he asked quietly, turning his head to look at his wife beside him.

Adrian and Avery also turned to look at her, their expressions ones of shock, fear and worry.

"I couldn't sleep, so I decided to come downstairs for a glass of milk," Joni began. "I glanced at the family room as I made my way into the kitchen and everything looked normal, perfectly normal," she said, as a fresh tear traveled down her face.

"I got my glass and I was sitting at the table thinking about you guys, when I heard something fall in the family room. I walked back through the foyer and this… this is what I saw." Her nose wrinkled as more tears trickled down her face.

Without warning, Joni walked up to Avery and pulled her into her arms. She put two fingers under her daughter's chin so she would look up at her. "I felt the pinch on the stairs," Joni told her. "I am so, so sorry I didn't believe you."

Avery clutched her mom, nuzzling her face into Joni's shoulder. "It's okay," she said in a muffled voice.

With grim faces, Tate and Adrian began to flip the furniture over. Joni volunteered to make everyone coffee and hot cocoa, since she assumed nobody would be able to sleep anytime soon. Avery watched her father and brother flip the television back over before she sat in front of it and restacked their movies.

As Adrian worked, he marveled at the feat. There wasn't a single thing left unturned in the family room. He stared up at the far wall of the room. His mother had insisted on getting a family portrait done every two years, and it had become a tradition to hang them all up in their old house in chronological order. Joni had taken the framed pictures and had staggered them along the wall in matching black frames. Each had been lifted up off the wall and turned upside down.

He stepped closer to the portraits, staring at his family's upside-down smiling mouths. They all looked as though they were frowning. The door to the half bath was open a few inches to the left of the portraits. On a whim Adrian decided to make sure everything was normal inside. He flipped the switch and the overhead light illuminated the bathroom. Hooked on the wall, above a towel rack, was a framed picture of some vibrant, blue belladonna flowers. It was upside down.

With dread in his heart, Adrian walked back to the foyer and into the kitchen. "The picture in the bathroom is upside down too," he told his mother. "We should probably check every room."

Joni had her back to him as she stood very still, hunched over a kitchen drawer. Adrian began to frown when he realized that his mother wasn't moving.

"Um, mom?" he murmured, taking a hesitant step forward. Was his mother going into shock?

At last, Joni swung around and looked at her son. Her eyes were alight with panic.

"All of the knives are gone," she whispered.

A chill began to flow over Adrian's body, starting with his spine. "All of them?" he asked.

Joni nodded. Adrian could tell by the way she caught her bottom lip between her teeth that she was trying not to cry again. He knew she was trying to keep it together for Avery's sake, as well as for his.

The Harrison family spent the rest of the early morning hours trying to integrate order and normalcy back into their lives. Each silently hoped that by righting the furniture they would somehow forget what they were up against. If it was just a wandering invisible entity, they could find a way to ignore it, lead ordinary lives. But it had shown a force, an ability they had not foreseen. It was playing with them, and they all knew it.

It was sometime around dawn when Tate and Adrian decided to take a break in the kitchen. They sat slumped around the table, flexing their aching muscles. Tate glanced at the analog clock that hung on the wall in the kitchen, looking frustrated. "It stopped the clock," he said, gritting his teeth.

Adrian's eyes moved from the analog clock down to the digital one that was displayed on the stove's interface. "It stopped all of them," he said quietly.

Tate leaned in and placed one of his large hands on his son's shoulder. His face was grim as he whispered, "Look, your mom is on edge and, frankly, I'm shocked that your sister hasn't hidden under a blanket in a closet somewhere. We need to keep our shit together, okay?"

Adrian nodded, and clapped his hand over his father's. "You got it, dad," he whispered back.

Tate smiled in gratitude and had opened his mouth to speak again when Avery let out a shriek from the family room. Both lunged from their seats and raced into the foyer. Joni immediately followed, practically tumbling down the steps to come to her daughter's aid.

Avery was standing in the middle of the foyer looking freaked out, but unharmed.

"What is it? What's wrong?" Tate demanded.

"Look!" the seven-year-old cried pointing down at the dark wood floor. Adrian, Joni and Tate hovered over her and stared at the ground.

It was where Joni had first stood as she looked into the family room and screamed. She had taken care of the glass shards, but had forgotten to wipe the milk up after she discovered the knives were all gone. The while liquid had fanned out when she had dropped her cup, but none of the family members had paid the mess any mind. Somehow, the milk had reformed into a puddle and had begun to take shape.

The family watched in shock and horror as beads of milk slid along the grains in the floor. There were dozens of them, each moving in different directions as if they were ants. Slowly, groups of them began to congeal together. Adrian squinted down at the mess, then took a step back.

"Oh," he said. His tone was flat and guarded.

"Oh what?" Avery demanded, tugging on the sleeve of his long-sleeved black t-shirt.

"Well… it's spelling out letters," he replied, attempting to sound nonchalant.

"What?!?" Joni cried. She leaned backward, studying the mess from down the bridge of her nose.

She began to see the thin, watery letters amidst the mess. The first was a long, sloppy J in the center of the foyer. Not far to the right was an A, immediately followed by a T and another A.

"It spells… JATA. Does anybody know what that means?" Joni said, glancing from Tate to Adrian.

Tate pulled at the sleeves of his thermal shirt, trying to suppress the wave of cold that overwhelmed him but had nothing to do with the temperature in the room.

"It's our initials," he said, almost as if to himself. He blinked at the letters over and over again, hoping that the next time he opened his eyes, it would all be gone. He glared at the mess and blinked about fifty times before he ran a hand through his messy black hair and sighed.

"We are going to need help," he added quietly. He did not need to look up at his family to know that they were nodding in agreement.

CHAPTER FIFTEEN

They reconvened in the kitchen. Each sat in their respective places at the kitchen table, looking as though the family dog had run away. Despite the chaos and the drama, Avery was half asleep, with her head nestled on her arms that were bent on top of the table.

Joni absentmindedly stirred a yellow coffee cup, either lost in thought or in a trance. Deep blue bags were visible under her eyes. Every once in a while her white terry cloth robe would expand and contract as she sighed.

Tate had already downed his own cup, but failed to look any more alive than his wife. He picked at a loose thread on his hunter-green flannel. He was desperate to take action, desperate to fix the situation. But how? And where to begin? It felt as if he needed to assemble a piece of furniture, and he could study each part and theorize on all the ways they might come together—but his instruction manual was in French.

Or perhaps German.

Adrian looked from one family member to the next. Their faces showed exhaustion and hopelessness, as if they had already conceded to... whatever it was that lurked within their house.

"I'm telling you, it's a poltergeist," he said with a brisk nod. "All of the evidence points to it. We haven't seen it because it isn't human. Ghosts take the form of orbs, or apparitions, but most of them are residual hauntings—"

"Residual hauntings?" Joni frowned as she sipped from her cup.

Adrian shifted forward in his seat so he could place his elbows on the table. "Yeah," he nodded. "It's basically when a place becomes haunted after a traumatic death occurred there. The ghosts are known to repeat the actions they took right before their death."

Tate groaned and rubbed at his eyes. "I don't follow."

"Okay, you know how in some places, people will say that they have seen ghosts walk around a building or house and not seem to realize that there is anybody around them?" Adrian pressed. "Well, that's a residual haunting. Say somebody had come into this house and had murdered Aunt Marie—"

"Adrian! That's terrible," Joni scoffed.

Her son causally flicked his hand. "I'm sorry, but it's just an example. Say Aunt Marie was standing in this very kitchen making tea when she heard someone knock on the door. Picture her walking from the kitchen to the front door, then suddenly being brutally killed the moment she opens the door."

Tate winced, staring into the dregs of his coffee cup. Joni sighed and took another sip from her own.

"Now, because the death was so unexpected and so violent, there's a strong possibility that the house is now haunted… just not in the way horror movies would have you believe," Adrian continued, feeling in his element. "Aunt Marie is not about to appear beside your bed, nor is she going to pop out at you when you least expect. If you saw her at all, it would be in the kitchen, seeing her ghostly form make tea and then walk to the front door before disappearing. Aunt Marie's soul is not in the house, but some of the energy of her death got left behind in residual form."

"Honey, that's interesting and all, but what does that have to do with our situation?" Joni asked as she began to chew on one of her nails.

"I'm trying to eliminate possibilities," he said with a meager shrug. "It directly interacts with us, so it is comprised of more than just lingering energy; thus, we can eliminate a residual haunting. But we have also confirmed that we can't see it with the naked eye, which goes against the theory that it is a dead person, now in ghost form."

"So…" Tate said, lacing his fingers together upon the table. "I'm assuming that leaves a poltergeist?"

Adrian nodded and brushed a strand of black hair out of his eyes. "I've been doing some research on them. From what I've read, each situation, or haunting, has been unique, but there are some things that seem characteristic of them. For example, moving furniture around."

Joni looked at her son with renewed interest. "Really?" she murmured.

"Yes," Adrian said gently. "There are numerous cases of poltergeists that have blown up in the media, as well as hundreds of cases that go unreported every year. Most, if not all, of those cases involved furniture being moved around and objects turning up in random places."

"Like the knives," Joni said.

"Exactly," Adrian nodded. "It's also a common characteristic for a poltergeist to leave messages to the living. In a lot of the cases I have read about, the poltergeists utilize anything that's left out in the open to write a message, be it paper and pencil, such as what has happened to me, or food, paint, all kinds of things."

Avery, who had been listening and watching her family with half-closed eyes, lifted her head up from the table to look at her brother.

"What about ones that pinch people on the stairs?" she asked timidly.

Adrian twisted up his mouth in thought. "I'll be honest with you, Av, there have been cases where poltergeists have been violent. I have yet to encounter any account where a supernatural being hid under the stairs to pinch people. But poltergeists have been known to attack people in some of the more severe cases I have read about."

Joni looked to her husband with an anxiety-ridden expression. He tried to give her a reassuring smile and reached out to take her left hand in his. He then turned to look back at his son with a determined expression.

"We need to figure out a way to take care of this. Before it gets any worse," he said grimly.

"Agreed," Joni and Adrian said in unison.

Suddenly, Joni held up the palm of her hand, swallowing hard. "I'd like to say something really quick. I wanted to tell each and every one of you how sorry I am that I didn't believe you. Is what we are dealing with absolutely crazy? Of course. If I had a neighbor who came up to me and insisted that they had an otherworldly spirit causing terror in their home, would I have believed it? Definitely not. But it's you guys," she said, looking from her husband to both her children. "I should have known better."

Avery leapt from her chair and went to hug her mother. "It's okay, Mom," she said, and smiled.

"Not once was I insulted that you didn't believe me. This whole ordeal is just… almost impossible to process," Tate said as he squeezed her hand on the table. "I knew you would come around; it was just a matter of when."

Adrian, too, gave her a warming smile. "It was logical for you to assume it was some kind of mental disorder or issue first," he said with a nonchalant shrug. "A haunting is not the first thing you think of—it's the last."

With that, he rose from his spot around the table and walked to the drawer that was to the immediate right of the refrigerator. It was the drawer where pens and batteries went to die. He sifted through an array of random office supplies until he found a scrap of paper and a pen that still managed to work. Adrian carried both items to the table and sat down back in his spot.

"I think the best thing to do now is brainstorm. We all realize we can't do this alone, that we need help. But who?" he asked as he readied the pen at the top of the paper.

Tate scratched at the nape of his neck with his free hand. "Well," he said. "I know priests typically handle cases of possession and demons and whatnot, but I don't think it would hurt to contact a church and see what they say."

"They might be able to offer advice, or connect us with some kind of service," Adrian agreed and began to scribble notes on the page.

"I could scope a few out," Joni volunteered as she drained the last of her cup. Avery still hovered behind her chair, casually playing with her mom's wavy brown hair. "I've been meaning to check out a few churches anyway, since Christmas is coming up soon."

"Mom… churches," Adrian repeated as he wrote it down. "I was thinking that I could check out the Ely Public Library and the library at school as well. Maybe I'll find suggestions on how to get rid of it," he said, jotting down his name upon the page.

"What about psychics?" Avery suggested. Her hands were entwined in Joni's hair as she tried to braid it. "People on those ghost hunting shows always have some psychic come with them to tell them things."

Joni frowned and turned her neck to look at her daughter. "I don't allow you to watch those shows," she said.

Avery gave her mom a rather devious smile. "I've seen them at Miranda's house," she admitted.

"Remind me to speak with Mrs. Shirpansky," Joni said, looking at Tate, who all in all seemed amused by his daughter's rebellious ways.

"Rules for Avery aside, that's actually not a bad idea," Adrian said, considering. "Okay, so yes, a psychic could either be genuinely gifted and could possibly provide some insight into the entity, or we find one who's a total fraud and we lose out on fifty bucks. Could be worth the risk."

"Well, since I haven't been assigned a task, I will volunteer to look for a psychic during my lunch breaks at work," Tate said as he rose and walked over to the Keurig on the counter.

Adrian wrote his father's name and duty onto the paper as Avery stomped her foot against the tile floor.

"No fair!" she cried. "That was my idea. Now I don't have anything!"

Anticipating such a reaction, Adrian carefully set his pen down and turned his body sideways into his chair. "Come here, Av," he said.

With pouty lips, Avery walked around the edge of the table until she stood in front of her brother. Their kneecaps almost touched through his gray cotton and her pink satin pajamas. Adrian took his sister's tiny hands into his own and looked at her with a solemn expression.

"Av, do you remember when Mom was being a stinker and she didn't believe us?" he asked.

Avery giggled for a moment and then nodded.

"You and me and Dad, we had to find a way to prove it to her, right? And to figure out everything we could know about the poltergeist, right?"

"Yes," she said, tilting her head to look up at him.

"I asked if you could try to write down everything you notice about the entity, remember? And I still need you to do that," he said, and gave her hands a quick squeeze before he left them go.

Avery wiggled her right big toe in the grout lines of the white tile floor. She lowered her head, suddenly unsure. "But what if it hurts me?" she whispered.

Adrian vehemently shook his head. "You don't need to get close to it, or even interact with it. Just if you sense it around the house, I want you to write it down, okay? We need to know where it goes, what it does. Can you be the brave sister I know you are and do this for me?"

A blush of pleasure blossomed across her cheeks. He knew his sister well. He knew she would not be content with some ordinary job, no… she needed a task that only she could perform.

"Okay," she said, beaming up at her brother.

Adrian smiled back and ruffled her already messy hair. "Glad we are all in this together," he said, and he meant it. The Harrisons had always been a fairly tight-knit family, but this experience brought bonding to a whole other level.

For the week that followed, each family member stayed busy, both with ordinary tasks and their assigned duties. Joni spent her lunchtimes eating salad by the family computer, writing down information about the local churches. While the ministry at each one seemed very friendly, the moment she spoke about her family's predicament, their attitudes toward her quickly changed.

"Nobody is professionally trained to handle exorcisms anymore," one priest had informed her. "It's an archaic practice and no longer relevant thanks to everything we know about mental disorders." He said the last remark rather pointedly.

Joni ground her teeth together and forced herself to smile. "I can understand that, but you see, it's not just one family member who is experiencing the presence in our house—it's all of us. We can't possibly all have the same disorder," she reasoned.

The priest laced his fingers behind his back and stared at her. They were in the sanctuary at St. Anthony's Catholic Church. Their conversation echoed against the cool stone walls and the stone ceiling thirty feet above their heads.

"Madam, if it is God's will, anything is possible," the priest replied, and turned his attention back to the altar at the front of the room.

Joni fumed about his snide remarks and mannerisms in the day that followed, but nothing could prepare her for how she was treated at the Community Church on Camp Street.

She had run into a pastor as she walked up the side-walk. "You're new here, aren't you? Welcome!" the pastor said. The sun reflected off his bald head in the chilly morning air.

"Hi, yes, as a matter of fact I am. I am interested in Sunday worship services, but I was also hoping you could provide advice as to a specific situation first…"

The spectacled pastor clapped his hands enthusiastically. "By all means, ask, ask," he said.

Only he wasn't so enthusiastic when she finished telling him her story. Instead, the pastor perpetually chuckled to himself and stared up at the sky as though God had personally sent Joni along to him for comic relief that day.

"Dear woman, there's no such thing as poltergeists," the pastor said. He used a sickly sweet smile, as if it could possibly disguise how patronizing he was being.

"There is," Joni replied, her tone flat. "It took all of our kitchen knives and it's hurting my family," she added.

The pastor squinted at her as though at any moment she would break down and admit she believed she was a purple alien from outer space. Joni kept her gaze steady and her expression severe. Perhaps if he realized how serious she was being…

The short, balding man chuckled again and shoved his wireframe glasses back up the bridge of his nose. "Ma'am, do you have kids at home? I'm betting the real culprit is a sullen child who didn't get the toy they wanted, or an emotional teenager who is angry about not getting that car."

Joni shook her head, feeling her patience unravel like a spool of thread. "No, listen to me," she snapped. "This isn't a matter of bratty children, or anything like that. We have a genuine paranormal entity in our house and we need help getting rid of it. So can you help or not?"

"No," the pastor said. "I'm afraid only a professional therapist could."

Joni stared down at the petite man. He continued to stare haughtily up at her, with a gleam in his eye that told her he believed she was far inferior to him and to his infinite wisdom.

"Well!" Joni cried throwing her hands up in an exaggerated shrug. "I guess you're just an idiot, then. Have a great day!"

And she marched back to her car, leaving the pastor to stare after her in indignation.

When the bell rang out after fourth period, Adrian quickly gathered up his textbooks and made his way to the library of Ely Memorial High School. It was lunch hour, and most of the students were down in the cafeteria. A handful of students were scattered here and there between the rows, or at one of the sturdy mahogany study tables that were lined up toward the front of the library. Each glanced up as Adrian entered before they quickly resumed their studies, hunched over their books.

Along the right-hand wall was a row of computers for the students to use. Hitching his messenger bag higher up on his shoulder, Adrian walked across the plush turquoise carpet and sunk down in front of a computer. The internet opened up to the library catalog, which was precisely what he was after.

With deft fingers, Adrian began to search through their occult collection. 'Collection' was a term he used loosely. The selection was meager at best, and most of the books that contained information about the occult were nothing but cheap paperback novels about some surly detective or other.

He scrolled further down with the mouse until a tan colored book with dark red letters caught his eye: *Poltergeists – Demons in the Home: Cleansing Your Home from Demonic Intruders*.

"That's the one," he said to himself. He grabbed a pen from his pocket and wrote down the book's call number on the back of his hand. Adrian got up and walked past the tables to the ceiling-high shelves, set one after another like dominos on the left-hand side of the library. Each shelf end had a plastic sleeve with call numbers listed on it in thick black lettering. He scanned the aisles until he found the shelving unit with call numbers in the 130 range.

Adrian inhaled the old, musty book smell as he scanned the numbers pasted on each book's spine. He glanced from his hand to the shelves, watching the numbers grow. He slowed down and gazed at the spot where the book should have been. He studied all of the surrounding titles in case it had been misplaced, but the book was nowhere to be found.

Puzzled, he walked back to the computer, where the catalog was still up. Right beside the call number was the word 'available.'

Adrian spent the next fifteen minutes scouring the shelving unit and conferring with the librarian at the reference desk. He tried to be patient as the pretty blonde librarian insisted that she, too, check the shelf.

"Strange," she said, peering at the books through her trendy, black-framed glasses. "It should be here, unless it has been put on hold, or has been taken into the back for circulation reprocessing. Let me go check."

But the young woman had no luck. Adrian thanked her and walked over to one of the study tables to wait out the rest of the lunch period. He placed his messenger bag in the maroon colored chair beside him and sat down.

Well, the public library would have to do—and he was certain it would have a much better collection to go through. He reached into the pocket of his jeans and fished out his cellphone. Perhaps if put the books on hold now, his mom could pick them up that afternoon.

He lightly touched the screen of his phone with his index finger as he looked for the public library's website.

"Ahhh-CHOOO!"

The sneeze, which was sudden and rather violent, made Adrian jolt in his seat. He glanced up to see a copper skinned boy wiping his nose with a Kleenex at the table across from him. He met Adrian's gaze.

"Sorry," he said sheepishly, and picked his book up from the table.

Adrian waved him off. "Bless you," he said, grinning.

He returned to his phone search for a few moments before he slowly looked up again. He could barely see the boy's eyes; his face was so engrossed in his book. His dark eyes flitted across the text as he gripped the edges of the book with both hands.

A book with a tan cover and dark red lettering.

Adrian slid his phone back into his pocket and slowly walked to the boy's table, wholly unsure of what he would even say.

"Hi," he began and smiled awkwardly.

The boy glanced up at him and smiled back. "Hello," he said.

"So… You're into poltergeists and what have you?" Adrian said, pointing to the title.

The boy flipped the book shut so he could read the title again. "I suppose so," he said, shrugging noncommittally.

Adrian nodded slowly. "I just started researching them myself."

"How come?"

Adrian's hazel eyes met the boy's black ones as he wrestled internally. On one hand, he had yet to make any friends at this school. The boy was so scrawny that it was quite likely he was only a freshman. But Adrian wasn't particularly at liberty to be picky. Did he really want to spill his problems onto someone who would most likely look at him as if he'd suddenly grown a second head?

And if he didn't divulge his family's dilemma? The boy seemed fairly apathetic about the subject, but that didn't mean he was ignorant about it. At the very least, if he explained what was going on, perhaps the boy would take pity on him and let Adrian check out the book.

After what felt like a small eternity, Adrian took a deep breath. "My house has been invaded by one," he mumbled.

This seemed to pique the boy's interest. He blinked up at Adrian as if sizing him up, then slowly closed the book and set it down on the wooden table. "By a poltergeist?" the boy asked.

Adrian grabbed the chair across from him and sat down. He put his hands flat against the table as if prepping for an interrogation. "Yes," he admitted.

The boy tilted his head. "Are you sure it's a poltergeist and not a ghost, though?"

"I'm pretty sure," Adrian nodded. "It stole all of the knives out of the kitchen and it likes to pinch our feet when we use the staircase after dark. Plus, it likes to antagonize me by leaving messages for me all over my room."

There. He had said it. Everything was out on the table. Adrian idly drummed his hands, expecting the boy to suddenly stand up from his chair and belly laugh right in his face.

Instead, the boy stroked his chin. "Yep, that sounds like a poltergeist, alright." He grinned and whistled. "I'm Ahmik, by the way," he added, extending a bony hand.

"Adrian," Adrian replied as he shook his hand.

"So, Adrian… are you trying to get rid of the pol- tergeist? I'm assuming yes," Ahmik said, grinning again.

Adrian ran a hand through his hair. "We want to, but we don't know what to do, or who to turn to. I mean, my parents are literally out right now talking to Ely priests and alleged psychics trying to see if anyone can help."

He sighed and marveled at how good it felt to speak to somebody so openly about what his family was going through. It had been well over a month since Avery had first mentioned the thing under the stairs. None of them had talked about it to anyone before. Somehow, it didn't seem prudent to give a new town that kind of ammunition against new neighbors.

Ahmik jerked his hand around as though waving a putrid smell away. "Forget the holy men, forget the late night infomercial psychics. What you need is a smudging ritual."

"A smudging ritual?" Adrian repeated. He ransacked his brain for the term, but found he didn't have any asso- ciations for it. "I'll be honest: I have no idea what that means."

Ahmik chuckled and slid the book to the empty side of the table. "I'm not surprised. It's a Native American ritual, and you're about as white as a sheet."

Adrian couldn't help but laugh in return. Maybe Ah- mik could become a friend after all. At least he was funny.

"Smudging is a ritual that Native Americans use to ward off negative energy or spirits," Ahmik explained, looking cheerful at the idea of sharing his knowledge with someone. "Basically, it is a stick made out of various herbs, like sage, that is meant to be burned in the infested area or by the affected person. You light the smudge stick, and the smoke it makes is supposed to carry those negative spirits away."

He lifted his hands and fluttered his fingers in the air before laughing again.

Adrian shifted uncomfortably in his seat. "Sounds like you don't take it very seriously," he said quietly.

Ahmik shook his head, looking slightly abashed. "No, I do," he insisted. "That's the real trick—you have to believe it will work for it to do so. Don't ever forget that. As a Sioux, I have seen numerous smudging rituals out on the reservation. It works."

Adrian felt his shoulders slump against the stiff, maroon chair. "I'm glad it seems to work and all, but is it something I could do? I have no idea where I would get a smudge stick around here, but if you can point me where to go, I'd really appreciate it, Ahmik."

The copper skinned boy looked at him again with that same assessing gaze. A silence fell over the two young men as one bore his eyes into the other and the other looked back, feeling more and more uncomfortable by the moment.

At last, Ahmik clapped his hands together. A girl who was writing in a notebook at an adjacent table flinched at the sudden noise.

The boy leaned forward with a mischievous grin on his face. "I'll tell you what. I like you. And I believe you when you say you've got a problem. My uncle Wapi is a Sioux elder, and if I tell him a friend of mine needs help, he could probably conduct the ritual for you."

Adrian knew that his jaw had dropped a few inches as he stared. He swore he could hear a fanfare triumphantly going off in his head. Had he actually found someone who could help?

"Are you serious?" he whispered.

The smirk on Ahmik's face slowly dissolved as he nodded. "Yeah," he said, his expression kind. "I don't know why, but there's something compelling me to help you. I can tell you need it."

Adrian shook his head a few times, then reached his hand out to shake Ahmik's once more. "You have no idea how grateful I am," he said. He reached into his messenger bag and pulled out a notebook and a pencil. He scribbled his name and phone number on one corner of a page and tore it off.

"Here," he said, handing it to Ahmik. "Please give this to your uncle. And please convey my gratitude if he accepts."

Ahmik took the scrap of paper between his index and middle finger and shoved it into the pocket of his pants under the table. "Sure thing, friend," he said, and smiled.

CHAPTER SIXTEEN

Adrian was amazed when he received a phone call from Uncle Wapi that very evening. The man spoke in a low, gravelly voice that seemed to warrant instant respect. He listened intently as Adrian paced around his bedroom, telling him everything that had happened at Lakeside.

When Wapi grew silent on the phone, Adrian began to panic. "We can pay you, you know. Whatever price you name. I mean, I didn't get the green light from my parents, but I'm sure they'd be onboard. I think," he finished lamely, smacking his palm against his forehead.

"No payment is necessary. Just give me your address, and I will gather my supplies. We will conduct the ritual tomorrow night," Wapi said.

No questions, no requests or polite diatribes about scheduling and convenience. Adrian would normally have found such finality to be irritating, and yet he somehow already knew that Wapi had only the best of intentions. His declaration that he would be conducting the ritual the following night was not a tribute to his ego.

How Adrian knew this, he did not know, nor did he question it. He spoke with Wapi a few more minutes, then concluded the phone call with a smile on his face.

His parents received the news with mixed emotions.

"We have no idea who this man is, or if he's dangerous, or anything at all," Joni said as she peeled a cucumber over the kitchen sink.

Adrian leaned against the counter beside her, watching the long green peels stick to the white porcelain. He chuckled a little to himself.

Joni jerked her head around, the peeler poised in mid-air in front of her. "What?" she demanded, her eyebrows lifted in exasperation.

Adrian shrugged. "Nothing, it's just… you act like we have another option available or something."

Joni pictured the small, balding pastor who had laughed outright in her face. "I know," she sighed. "I know."

Thankfully, Tate was more accepting of the idea, and it was he who opened the glass paneled front door for Wapi when he arrived at eight the following evening.

The man who stood on the front porch had copper colored skin like his nephew, but his was covered in various lines and wrinkles. Two thick black braids, which started above his ears, trailed down either side of his face nearly to his waist. He wore a tan button-down shirt and a jean jacket.

"Hi," Tate said, slightly abashed. "You must be Wapi. Please come in." He held the door out wider and waved Wapi inside.

Joni, Adrian and Avery all waited in the foyer, ready to greet and thank their guest for coming. Wapi was everything that Adrian had imagined him to be while they had talked on the phone. He was a large man with broad shoulders, but he stepped into the foyer with ease and grace.

Joni held her hand out to him, and he took it. "I'm Joni," she said. "That's Tate that you just met, and these are our kids, Adrian and Avery. Thank you so much for coming, Wapi."

Her tone was gracious and sincere. Wapi nodded and gave her a soft smile. "Ahmik seemed confident that your family needed help. I am happy to provide that help. May I look around?"

"Please," Tate said, gesturing toward the family room. "By all means."

The Harrisons slowly followed Wapi as he made his way through the house, stopping in each room of the first floor. He peered up at each corner of the ceiling, his face stoic. After he had looped through the kitchen, bathroom and laundry room, Wapi made his way back to the family room.

"Yes," he said, whacking his knuckle against the wall. "I feel it all around us, swimming in the air like a toxin," he murmured. "I can feel its presence."

The elderly man closed his eyes and placed both hands, palm up, in front of him. He concentrated on his breathing, letting his hands rise and fall with each breath. Avery sat on the floor beside the television, staring up at the man with her mouth open. Adrian leaned against the upright piano that sat, often neglected, in the corner of the room. Tate and Joni watched Wapi from beside the black leather couch, their hands entwined together as they waited, hopeful.

Wapi suddenly stopped mid-breath and opened his eyes wide. "It knows I am here and it does not like it. Not one bit."

As if on cue, the rectangular glass coffee table jumped off the ground a few inches before it came thudding back down on the floor. Avery screamed and scrambled to get to her mother. She clung to Joni's long, plum colored duster with both fists, staring at the coffee table in unwavering fear.

Wapi remained tranquil and began chanting under his breath as he walked around the perimeter of the room. Adrian stared in wonder as every piece of furniture, including the couch and piano, leapt a few inches into the air as he passed by. Each member of the Harrison family flinched as one by one the furniture came crashing back to the ground again, smashing to the floor with loud thuds.

Wapi moved to the center of the room and remained still. He indicated the couch with a steady hand. "Please, sit down," he said, looking from Joni and Tate to Adrian in the corner.

The family squished together on the couch, glancing down at the black leather with wary faces. They expected the couch to rise into the air again at any given moment.

When they were all settled, Wapi laced his fingers together in front of him. "There is no denying that a malignant spirit lingers here," he said, looking to each family member with gravity. "For many centuries, my people, the Sioux Indians, have encountered these phantom foes and have developed a cleansing ritual to rid homes of such entities."

He unlaced his thick, wrinkled fingers and reached into his shirt pocket. He pulled out a short, wide bundle of dried green herbs, strung together with thread. Adrian knew at once that he was looking at a smudge stick.

"I want to perform a ritual called smudging," Wapi said, holding the smudge stick in his open palm so the Harrisons could see it. "I will light the stick and I will go through each room of the house with it. As the stick smolders from the flame, a dense smoke will issue from it and grow heavy in each room. This smoke will envelop the dark entity and all of its negative energy and will carry it away, out of the house."

He looked at Adrian, his expression severe. "The poltergeist has already felt my presence and perceives me as a threat. It will not like the ritual, and it will try to use force to prevent the ritual's completion. I must warn each and every one of you that poltergeists are violent, otherworldly beings without any regard for human life. It is not —nor has it ever been—human. It does not know the human constructs of kindness, forgiveness or goodness. Never expect it to show mercy," he said softly, shaking his head.

"Are you ready?" he asked.

Adrian looked from his sister to his parents. Their eyes were wide with nerves and their skin appeared chalky and pale. Nobody seemed ready, but they each made eye contact with each other and nodded.

"We are ready," Tate said, dipping his chin to his chest.

Wapi nodded back and pulled out a white lighter from his back pocket. "Then let us begin," he said. He rolled his thumb along the metal crank of the lighter. A small orange flame ignited and he slowly turned the edge of the smudge stick into it. A dense, light gray smoke began to seep from the stick and waft into the air all around them.

The moment the smoky tendrils reached the ceiling, all hell broke loose.

CHAPTER SEVENTEEN

The gray velvet curtains that hung on each of the windows in the family room snapped closed of their own volition. Joni watched in horror, covering her mouth with her hands in shock.

Suddenly, the piano, an old wooden upright one, began to play by itself. Keys were pounded down by the unseen force. The notes were erratic and frenzied, lending to the emotional turmoil of the scene.

A harsh crash had Joni and Tate running to the kitchen. They stood in shock as one by one the cabinets flew open. Plates began to fly off the shelves, crashing and shattering against the cold tile floor. Cups rattled, then flew through the air, smashing against the refrigerator across the room.

"Please return to me," Wapi called from the family room. They could barely hear him over the noise. Joni and Tate walked back through the foyer and found their kids standing in front of Wapi, ducking as various baubles and trinkets were thrown around the room.

Wapi held up the smudge stick. "I must cleanse you all with the smudge stick, or else you could be vulnerable to attack."

Avery gave a soft whimper and took a step closer to Wapi, silently volunteering to go first. Wapi smiled kindly down at her and traced the outline of her body with the stick, letting the smoke wrap around her. He bent at the waist so he could look into her wide, panicked brown eyes.

"It's okay now. You are protected," he said, and nodded.

Avery nodded back, then ran to the couch, where she tucked herself underneath one of the armrests, on the floor.

"Mrs. Harrison," Wapi said, motioning her forward with his fingers.

"I will cleanse you next," he murmured as she stepped in front of him. "In order to keep your family safe, you must first be safe."

Joni nodded, fighting back tears that began to pool in her eyes. She watched as the picture frames on the far left wall began to rattle and fall to the ground. No, not fall, she thought to herself. They were being thrown. She could hear the tinkling sound of their glass cracking from the force.

Wapi traced her body with the smoke, then told her he was finished. Joni turned around and crouched beside her daughter, letting Avery crawl onto her lap and hide her face with her hair as she leaned into her mother's chest.

Tate was closer to Wapi than Adrian was, so Wapi gestured for him to come forward. He was holding the smudge stick up near Tate's temples, ready to begin cleansing him, when a deafening roar radiated from somewhere in the kitchen.

Adrian raced through the foyer.

"Wait!" Wapi barked after him, but Adrian did not hear him over the din all around them.

The moment Adrian stepped into the kitchen, he knew the sound had come from the basement. Everything suddenly seemed to fit together… why the poltergeist insisted that Avery play with it in the basement, why he and his family were most vulnerable to its attacks while on the stairs—which were directly above the ones leading underground.

It lived in the basement.

Adrian hesitated for a moment, then tentatively reached out and placed his hand on the long silver knob on the basement door. The latch clicked and Adrian slowly pulled the door open. He leaned a little forward, looking down into the dark, dank basement. It was almost impossible to see down there without the lights on.

He learned in a little more, reaching out to pull the cord of the light bulb on the ceiling above his head. The tips of his fingers were mere millimeters away when a heavy force gathered behind him and surged forward.

Adrian yelped as he lost his footing and pitched forward, looking down at the steps below as they careened toward him. He landed on his head, then tumbled forward, his body rolling over. The harsh edges of the steps pressed into various parts of his body as he continued to tumble.

With one last thud, he felt cold concrete underneath him. "Shit," he growled to himself. He wiggled his limbs around experimentally, feeling as though he had just been trampled by a raging elephant.

Adrian rubbed a sore spot on his forehead as he looked up the stairs. The light from the kitchen bathed the doorway with a warm, yellowy glow. As he looked, two figures appeared at the top of the staircase. Tate and Wapi were both looking down at him with concerned faces.

"Adrian? Are you alright?" Tate asked, his voice strained with anxiety.

"I'm alright," Adrian called up to him. Groaning as he got to his feet, Adrian placed his right foot on the first step and watched in horror as the basement door slammed shut, leaving him in utter darkness.

"Adrian!" Tate bellowed through the door. He could hear his father frantically rattling the doorknob and pounding his fists against the door. "Adrian!" he called out again, with a tone of helplessness.

"I'm okay!" Adrian hollered back. "At least, I hope I am," he whispered to himself as he turned to look at the interior of the basement. He may as well have been swimming at the bottom of the ocean. Everything was pitch black.

The longer he stood in the darkness, the more aware he became of the fact that he wasn't alone in the basement. He stared into the farthest corner of the room, feeling a sense of irrepressible dread bloom inside his stomach. Suddenly he recalled his conversation with Avery—about how she could feel it moving around the house.

Adrian stood still, listening and feeling the entity watch him from the corner. He didn't need to see the poltergeist to know that it was incredibly pleased with how things had panned out. Part of it focused its malignant energies on the basement door, keeping it firmly shut against Tate and Wapi.

But most of it was focused on Adrian, studying him.

Biding its time.

THE INHERITANCE · 161

CHAPTER EIGHTEEN

Tate pounded his fist against the door and sighed. He turned to look at Wapi, who quickly ducked as a bowl came flying past his head before smashing onto the floor.

"What do we do?" Tate asked him, holding his hand against the doorknob.

Joni and Avery suddenly appeared in the doorway from the foyer, looking at the two men with puzzled expressions.

"What was that noise? And where did Adrian go?" Joni asked. Avery continued to cling to her, staring up at her father and Wapi from around Joni's hips.

Tate sighed. "Adrian is stuck in the basement," he muttered.

Joni bobbed her head forward in disbelief. "What?" she said, blinking several times.

"The poltergeist tricked him," Wapi said in his gravelly voice. "That noise was made to get Adrian to the basement. The entity pushed him down the stairs and forced the door closed." He motioned to the door, looking grim.

"Oh my God, my son…" Joni whispered, feeling her eyes sting. She fluttered her hands out on either side of her as she panicked. "Is he okay? Did he get hurt in the fall? Oh my God."

Tate rushed to her side, cupping her face in his large hands. "Hey, hey," he said, forcing her to make eye contact with him. "It will be okay, Adrian will be okay. I promise you. He didn't get hurt from the fall, but it's pitch black down there and all of us need to pull together and find a way to get him out."

He turned back to face Wapi, looking bleak. "Any suggestions?" he asked.

Wapi stared at the door as he slowly stroked his chin. "I think the only way we can carry on is if Adrian conducts the cleansing ritual himself, down in the basement. That is the entity's dwelling place, where it draws power and is at its strongest," he said, ignoring Joni's soft cries. "If he can perform the ritual down there... it might be powerful enough to make the poltergeist disappear for good."

Tate nodded, his mouth a thin line across his face. "Just tell us how we can help and we'll do it," he said fiercely.

Wapi looked up at Tate and gave him a sympathetic expression. "I'm afraid it is up to Adrian now. All you and your family can do is wait. Wait and pray."

Tate nodded slowly as Joni reached out and clutched at his hand.

The smudge stick, which still fumed in Wapi's hand, made smoke gather above their heads. With stiff movements, Wapi sank to his knees and crouched low to the ground, looking at the gap underneath the door.

"It should be enough," he murmured, half to himself. He carefully placed the smudge stick on its side on the floor and used his index finger to push it through the gap.

"Adrian! Feel your way up the steps. The smudge stick is on the first step," Wapi bellowed through the small crack under the door.

"Okay," Adrian hollered back. He reached out with both hands, feeling the air around him as he cautiously shuffled his feet against the cold concrete floor. He moved forward until his toes rammed against the solid mass that was the bottom step.

Ignoring the pain, Adrian slowly crawled up the steps until he saw the red orange embers of the smudge stick, faintly glowing on the uppermost stair. Gingerly he picked it up, coughing slightly as the smoke overwhelmed his nostrils.

"Okay," he coughed. "I got it. Now what?"

"You must first cleanse yourself with the stick, starting at the top of your head and working your way down," Wapi said through the door. "Keep your mind clear and your focus on overcoming the entity as you cleanse, Adrian.

Adrian stood on the step on the opposite side of the door. The embers were faint, but they gave the faintest orange glow to the staircase. "Okay," he murmured to himself. "Clear mind…"

He closed his eyes and imagined the entity in his mind. He pictured what it might have looked like had it been visible. He imagined it having a thick, gray skin and grotesque features. He pictured the poltergeist as being weak, as being vulnerable, as being nothing more than a speck of cosmic dust, floating aimlessly and harmlessly through the universe.

With steady hands, Adrian lifted the smudge stick and placed it near his forehead. He let the smoke work its way around his head until he moved to his arms, then on to his legs. He looked down at what he could see of his body, wondering if he should feel any different. Should he feel safer? Stronger?

He let himself wonder briefly before shaking his head in dismissal. They were herbs, not super powers.

"Alright," he yelled under the door. "What do I do now, Wapi?"

Looking under the door, he saw Wapi's wrinkled brown face looking back at him. His dark eyes were stern, yet patient. "Now you must go to each corner of the basement and smoke them, from top to bottom," the Sioux said.

Adrian swallowed hard. "Even the corner where it now lurks?" he asked, unable to disguise the fear in his voice.

Wapi looked at him, his brow wrinkled in sympathy. "Yes, I'm afraid so," he murmured. "But you must be sure to cleanse that corner last, so the entity feels cornered in an otherwise purified space. Understand?"

Adrian nodded, his expression grim. "Yes, Wapi. I understand," he said.

"Adrian?"

The seventeen-year-old looked to see the warm brown eyes of his little sister peering at him through the crack.

"Hey, Av," he said, forcing his mouth into a false smile.

"The thing... it's down there with you," she said, looking worried.

Adrian sighed. "I know it is."

"Don't let it win," she said.

He studied her expression. Her long, straight eyebrows were arched in such a way that was reminiscent of a look his mother often gave him. It was a look of love. And of pride.

CHAPTER NINETEEN

"Never," he told her, and gave her a genuine smile. With that, he turned and slowly made his way down the steps, reaching with his foot out to ensure he had touched the bottom.

The basement was still impossibly dark, but the embers allowed him to see the smudge stick, as well as the hand that held it. He could still feel the entity, lurking, watching him from behind his parents' belongings. He hadn't spent any time in the basement since they had moved, but he had helped his father with the grueling process of unpacking their stuff and placing it onto wide gray industrial shelving units. Three flanked each wall of the basement, filled with all manner of things. Toys and dolls Avery refused to let her mother donate, tax documents and tennis rackets.

"Why are we keeping all this junk?" he remembered his father asking his mother, back in their old house in Deland. They had one of the few houses in the Florida neighborhood that had a basement. Tate once had plans to convert the space into a home gym, but over time the space was taken over by objects and mementos Joni found it hard to discard.

"Because we might need all of this junk someday!" she had replied, tossing a pair of musty bowling shoes into a cardboard box.

Adrian felt and shuffled his way to the nearest corner. That was all that was there in the basement: Adrian, a poltergeist, and a whole lot of useless junk that would in no way help him battle a supernatural being.

His hands wobbled in the air until they felt a rough stone wall in front of him. Adrian shifted to his right, dragging his hands along the wall until he found the corner.

"Okay," he said. "Here goes."

He closed his eyes and raised the smudge stick towards his face once more.

He could feel the poltergeist grow enraged behind him. The moment the stick was near Adrian's forehead, boxes, bags and objects began to fall off the shelving units. Some fell to the ground with various thuds, whacks and clonks. Others careened through the air, knocking into Adrian as he tried to concentrate.

"I will not give in to you," he whispered. "I will not let you take control." He moved the smudge stick from his forehead up toward the ceiling, dragging the stick down along the corner. He inhaled the strange aroma of smells layered in the smoke. It was his only sense of comfort, down in the dark.

The entity continued to throw objects around the room in a fury. After the first corner was finished, Adrian grabbed the wall with his left hand and slid his palm against the bumpy surface, making his way to the next corner.

After a few steps he felt cold metal against his fingers. He groped for the shelf's edges, moving his body around its corner. The actual shelves were smooth and slick under his hand. He continued to shuffle along until he felt a small gap, indicating he had walked past one unit to the next.

Which was when the shelves themselves began to rattle and shake. Adrian stared up in fear as they bounced violently and began to tip forward. He ran in a straight line as the shelves began to crash to the floor behind him.

Adrian kept running until his hands and knees collided with another wall. He pressed his body flat against the stone as the shelving unit beside him toppled forward. He remembered reading about a poltergeist's abilities in his room. One paranormal investigator had written that poltergeists, much like ghosts, required energy to interact with the world of the living. He had no way to discern how much energy the poltergeist used to push industrial shelves around, but he was thankful the entity wasn't faster about it. He had been a mere ten inches from being caught and crushed by the last one.

With deep breaths, Adrian grappled for the wall and stumbled into the corner. He didn't realize he was trembling until he held up the smudge stick and saw it quaver in front of him. He began to run the smudge stick along the wall, but found he couldn't focus. The entity seemed to expand in the darkness, as though it were absorbing more energy from the room and the objects all around it. Deep in his gut, Adrian knew it was gearing up for something far worse than toppling shelves.

As Adrian reached the bottom of the corner with the smudge stick, he felt the poltergeist advance upon him. It swept forward like an invisible cloak, rushing towards him. Instinctually, Adrian crouched and made his body as small as possible. He hunched his back and used his arms to shield the smudge stick against the wave of cold that washed over him.

The thing knew Adrian was powerless without the miniscule embers glowing and sizzling on the smudge stick. He cupped his left hand around the top of the stick as he turned around and pressed his back into the uneven wall. Dragging the back of his t-shirt against the wall, he inched his way to the third corner of the room. With every inch, he could feel the presence of the poltergeist intensify. He stared into the farthest fourth corner of the basement and felt his skin turn cold with trepidation.

He was halfway to the third corner when he began to feel a thousand fingers touching his skin, all over his body. It was as if he was covered with a hundred phantom hands, pinching his skin between their thumbs and index fingers. He snapped his eyes shut, trying to transcend the pain.

Adrian trudged along, letting his back scrape against the wall. Despite the darkness, he knew that swollen, red welts were beginning to form along his arms and legs. His clothes seemed irrelevant.

"Keep going," he whispered to himself. "Finish this."

His pain sharpened with each passing moment, but he endured. By the time he reached the third corner, it felt as though someone had stuck him with a thousand needles, leaving their thin metal points deep in his flesh.

He tucked his body as far into the corner as it would go, using his shoulders to protect the flame. Adrian quickly raised the smudge stick high up on the wall, wanting to complete this portion of the room before the thing gathered enough energy to retaliate.

As he began to lower the herbs along the wall, each of his welts seemed to go up in flames. He cried out at the pain, letting his body fall against the cool stone surface. Adrian had always had a high pain tolerance, but his supernatural wounds were unbearable. His eyes grew wet as he struggled to breathe, struggled to remain standing against the severity of the pain.

With a long, gasping breath, Adrian dragged the stick along the wall. He did not draw breath again until the entire corner had been smoked out. He stood to his full height again and wondered if he was experiencing how it felt to catch on fire.

He crept along the last wall, his concentration on each step that he took and each breath he drew into his lungs. As he took one step and then another, he was shocked to feel that the pain of his welts did not intensify. If anything it seemed to dull. Had the poltergeist used up all the energy it could obtain?

"Last one," he whispered to himself, catching the skin of his palm against the many imperfections of the wall. He trudged forward, growing increasingly alarmed that he wasn't riddled with more pain. He could feel the poltergeist hovering in the corner he approached.

Something about it felt… off. It was almost as if the thing was hibernating. Adrian could feel its presence, but in a fleeting, abstract sort of way. Was it because of the smudging ritual? Was the entity finally growing weak?

The moment Adrian reached the fourth corner, he knew that he had been dead wrong. The poltergeist flared up and surged forward. It had been gathering energy— energy it now used against Adrian in full force.

He cried out in horror as he felt his body being lifted off the ground and thrown through the air. He cried out again as his back slammed against the wall closest to the staircase. His eyes grew wide as he looked down at his feet, which were dangling in the air. The poltergeist had him pinned high up on the wall.

Adrian gritted his teeth, trying to pry his torso off the wall with all of his might. But he couldn't budge. The otherworldly being continued to watch him as he struggled. Something within Adrian told him that the entity was laughing at him. That the entity thought of him as a mere toy.

"Wapi!" he roared, trying to force his voice to carry up the stairs. "Wapi, help! I'm stuck!"

His attention quickly turned to the fourth corner again, as the entity began to slink toward him. Adrian could feel the force of the being stretching toward him through the dark, spreading itself wide as though it were a blanket, come to smother him to death.

"Adrian!"

It took all of his strength to crane his head towards the staircase. "Wapi! I'm stuck, help!" he yelled again.

He could hear a faint rustling on the floor above him. Was that his mother, crying out at the sound of his voice? He heard the ceiling creak softly above his head, and then the distant sound of someone thudding against the floor.

"Adrian," Wapi shouted. "Adrian, you must listen to me, now. The ritual holds no power unless you believe that it holds power. Close your eyes! Concentrate!"

The seventeen-year-old forced himself to take a deep breath and close his eyes. He focused on the potent, rich smell of the smoke undulating in the air all around him. He imagined each of his family members in his mind, hovering above the staircase, desperately trying to reach him and put their turmoil to rest.

He thought back over the last month and a half, from the time his sister first casually mentioned the thing beneath the stairs, to feeling its phantom touch against his very own skin.

At first he had been, naturally, skeptical of his sister's tales. Adrian was a man of science. Whatever could not be explained away with logic was not within the realm of possibility to him. He had taken his sister's story as a falsehood, and therefore he had not perceived the entity that lived in the house with them.

But as he had opened his mind to the possibility, he had become more susceptible to encountering the spirit itself. It became a presence to him because he accepted the idea that such a presence was possible.

I gave it power when I chose to believe in it, he marveled. And once he knew that, he knew what he had to do.

Adrian's eyes flickered open. He stared at where he knew the poltergeist was, slithering toward him like a relentless snake. He continued to feel the sharp pain of the welts along his body, but suddenly the pain became secondary. If he concentrated hard enough he could turn the pain off with a switch. He took a deep breath and focused on the phantom mass flowing towards him. It crept over closer, but Adrian no longer felt fear. The poltergeist stared at him and Adrian stared right back.

"I give you power because I believe in you," he told the entity. "And I will give you no more."

The supernatural being surged forward but veered off towards the ceiling the moment it came close to him. He yelped as he felt himself fall free from the wall, onto the floor. The basement was still enveloped in inky blackness, but Adrian no longer needed the walls to navigate. He was not afraid.

He ran forward through the darkness until he finally stumbled into the fourth and farthest corner of the basement. He thrust the smudge stick upward and watched as smoke dispersed in small ringlets. He dragged his hand down the corner and felt the poltergeist begin to weaken.

The entity let out a low-pitched, inhuman growl as it floundered about the room. It reached out in all directions, attempting to regain strength from books, picture frames —anything that gave off a pulse of energy. But Adrian could feel it mentally recoil, sensing that each object had been cleansed with the herbal smoke.

It howled again as it began to dissolve into the dark air around it. Wapi had been right. The poltergeist had nowhere safe to go. Adrian watched in fascination, sensing the destruction of the entity rather than seeing it.

He stared around the basement, watching as the room grew two shades lighter than he had ever seen it. He felt his mood grow light and carefree, void of all worries. Even his very bones felt lighter inside the muscle and tissue that encased them.

Adrian continued to stand in the dark basement until he blinked and looked around. It was gone. There wasn't a single trace of the entity left.

CHAPTER TWENTY

Adrian knew that if he touched the doorknob to the basement, it would yield for him. He thrust the door forward, practically spilling onto the floor of the kitchen.

"Adrian!" Avery shrieked, flinging herself into her brother's arms. Caught by surprise, Adrian buckled under his sister's weight and crumpled to the ground. He threw his arms around her, laughing.

"I'm alright, I'm alright!" he said, chuckling.

Avery looked up at him, her eyes wide with alarm and curiosity. "Is it gone?" she whispered. "Is it really gone?"

He looked down at her. He still marvelled at how his seven-year-old sister had handled the infestation. Adrian could not imagine what it must have been like, feeling and sensing this dark, otherworldly being wandering around the house and having nobody who believed she was telling the truth. He couldn't imagine the overwhelming sense of fear she must have felt, staring down that long, ominous staircase, wondering if she would be attacked again. Attacked and chided for speaking out about it.

"It is," he whispered back. "It's gone. And I could have never gotten rid of it without you." He smiled down at her and reached a hand up to ruffle her tousled brown hair.

Avery let out a sigh of relief and giggled into her small, pale hands.

Joni and Tate were not far behind, throwing their arms around their son. He could feel his mother's tears soak into the shoulder of his sweater as she held him in his arms, stroking his hair with his fingers.

Adrian looked up from his mom's shoulder to see Wapi leaning against the counter by the sink with his arms crossed. He looked down at Adrian and smiled, dipping his chin towards his chest.

Everyone, including the Sioux, later gathered around the kitchen table to discuss what had happened. Adrian recounted everything that had happened to him in the basement. He watched Joni's, Tate's and Avery's faces as they ranged from fear to shock to delight. The air in the kitchen felt light and airy—devoid of any unseen, irre-pressible force.

After Adrian's story, Wapi cleared his throat and glanced at every member of the Harrison family. "Adrian's cleansing ritual was a success," he murmured quietly. "I no longer feel the poltergeist within this house."

"Me either," Avery said, smiling at the older man, tossing her legs back and forth under the table.

"Wapi, do you know where the entity might have come from?" Joni asked, flicking her palm upward. "My Aunt Marie lived here for some thirty years and never once mentioned anything unusual or paranormal happening. And if you had known my aunt, you would know she would have greatly enjoyed the drama of it all."

The Native American slowly stood up from the table and meandered around the kitchen, letting his eyes wander from the quartz countertops to the stainless steel refrigerator.

"Did your aunt decorate this house?" he asked, turning to look back at Joni.

She leaned onto the table, resting her chin in her hands. "If you can call it that," she grinned. "After our family decided we should move here, I thought the house would be the perfect opportunity to showcase my interior design skills, so I redecorated."

Wapi nodded, his braids shifting up and down on his tan colored shirt. "It was extensive?" he asked.

She tilted her head in thought. "Well, most of it was cosmetic, but we did have some of the wiring re-done. We also insulated the attic a bit more."

Again Wapi nodded. He turned to face the family with his hands laced in front of him. "I believe that is what triggered the entity," he said.

"What?" Tate said, looking bewildered as he bounced Avery up and down upon his lap at the table. "Where's the correlation?"

Wapi made his way back to the table and sat down. "It's actually quite common," he said, giving Tate a slightly amused smile. "I don't need to tell you that this house is old, very old. The energy of many different people, many different events, has all gotten trapped inside of its walls. And when you attempt to renovate a place like that, you disrupt the energy and the spirits that dwell within. Sometimes it results in a single event haunting... other times it becomes a long battle, a fight for one's home and for one's family."

Joni slumped in her chair. "So this is my fault," she said bitterly.

Wapi reached out and placed a wrinkled hand upon her shoulder. "It is not your fault that you wished to make a happy home for your family," he insisted.

Joni looked up at him and smiled in gratitude.

"Don't blame yourself, Jo," Tate said, reaching for her hand across the table. "There's no way you could have known. None of us could have. It doesn't matter how it started, it just matters how it ended. With all of us safe." He looked down at his daughter, who was still fidgeting around in his lap, and pressed his lips to her hair.

"Just let this be a lesson learned," Wapi said, looking to each of them. "Spirits are real. They're real and powerful, and not all of them are inherently good. Some were once living but are no longer, while others have never been human at all. The important thing is to never give the entity power over you."

He turned to look at Adrian, who sat quietly at the table. "Adrian, you realized this complex lesson while trapped against a wall, battling a poltergeist. I am impressed by your wisdom. You saved your entire family's lives tonight."

Adrian looked from Wapi to Avery, then to his parents. Each of them was beaming at him unabashedly. Joni wiped at her eyes. He shook his head, but a smile remained on his face.

"Actually, Wapi... it was my family who saved mine," he said.

Over the next few weeks, the Harrison family relearned what it was like to lead ordinary, human lives. The house was calm and quiet. Nobody feared walking down the stairs after dark. And Joni smiled every time she opened the cutlery drawer and found that all of the knives were tucked neatly inside.

Avery continued to make friends at school. Sarah still refused to talk to her, but Avery was too busy socializing to even notice. On the weekend that followed the ritual, she invited a red-haired girl named Megan to come play at the house. Megan wound up staying the night. Adrian helped them make an elaborate fort in the family room.

When Avery woke up the following morning, Megan was still there beside her.

Tate made it a new habit to sip his morning coffee while standing in the middle of the backyard. Avery insisted that the neighbors would find him silly, standing out there in his robe every day. But Tate didn't care. He'd just sip at his coffee and stare out at the lake, patiently waiting for spring to arrive.

Adrian became fast friends with Ahmik. He no longer spent his days alone, contemplating what his future might hold. He decided he wanted to follow in Aunt Marie's footsteps and become the next writer in the family. He decided his first task would be to write a book about his family's experience with the poltergeist.

Joni threw herself into her interior design business and began to gain a pool of clients. She used Lakeside as her work sample, and many women and men of Ely flocked to her, asking her for estimates. After each contract was signed, Joni would take Wapi to her client's home and perform a smudging ritual.

Just in case.

AUTHOR NOTES

FREE: Three "Spine Tinglers"
SHORT CREEPY STORIES

Building a relationship with my readers is the very best thing about writing. I occasionally send newsletters with details on new releases, special offers and other bits of news relating to hauntings and thrillers.

I'm giving away THREE short creepy stories - each 8K words (about an hour to read) - FREE.

Sign up right now and be the FIRST to hear about all activities and releases. Please visit
www.JamesMMatheson.com for more details.

Enjoy this book? You can make a big difference

I sincerely hope you enjoyed my book. If you did, please consider leaving a brief review on Amazon. Reviews are my most powerful secret to spreading the word.

I'm proud of the fact that I have a large list of loyal readers. I don't have the budget that the big publishing houses have, but I do have you.

Please leave a review wherever you purchased this book from.

Thank you in advance for doing so.

ABOUT THE AUTHOR

James M. Matheson is a storyteller. His grade seven class took a trip to a northern pioneer village, where, on talent night he shared a story about a table possessed by spirits that terrified his classmates. He has written and told scary stories ever since. He lives in the southwest USA with his wife.

Made in the USA
Middletown, DE
09 December 2017